BORGIA OF THE GLADES

A GIRL LEFT BEHIND

LAURA DRUMHELLER

AMAZON

Author: Laura Drumheller

Title: *Borgia of the Glades*

Title: *The Late Great Cakes of the United States*

Pen Name: Peregrine Maxson

Cover Design: Britney Drumheller

Editor: Cynthia Couture

❀ Formatted with Vellum

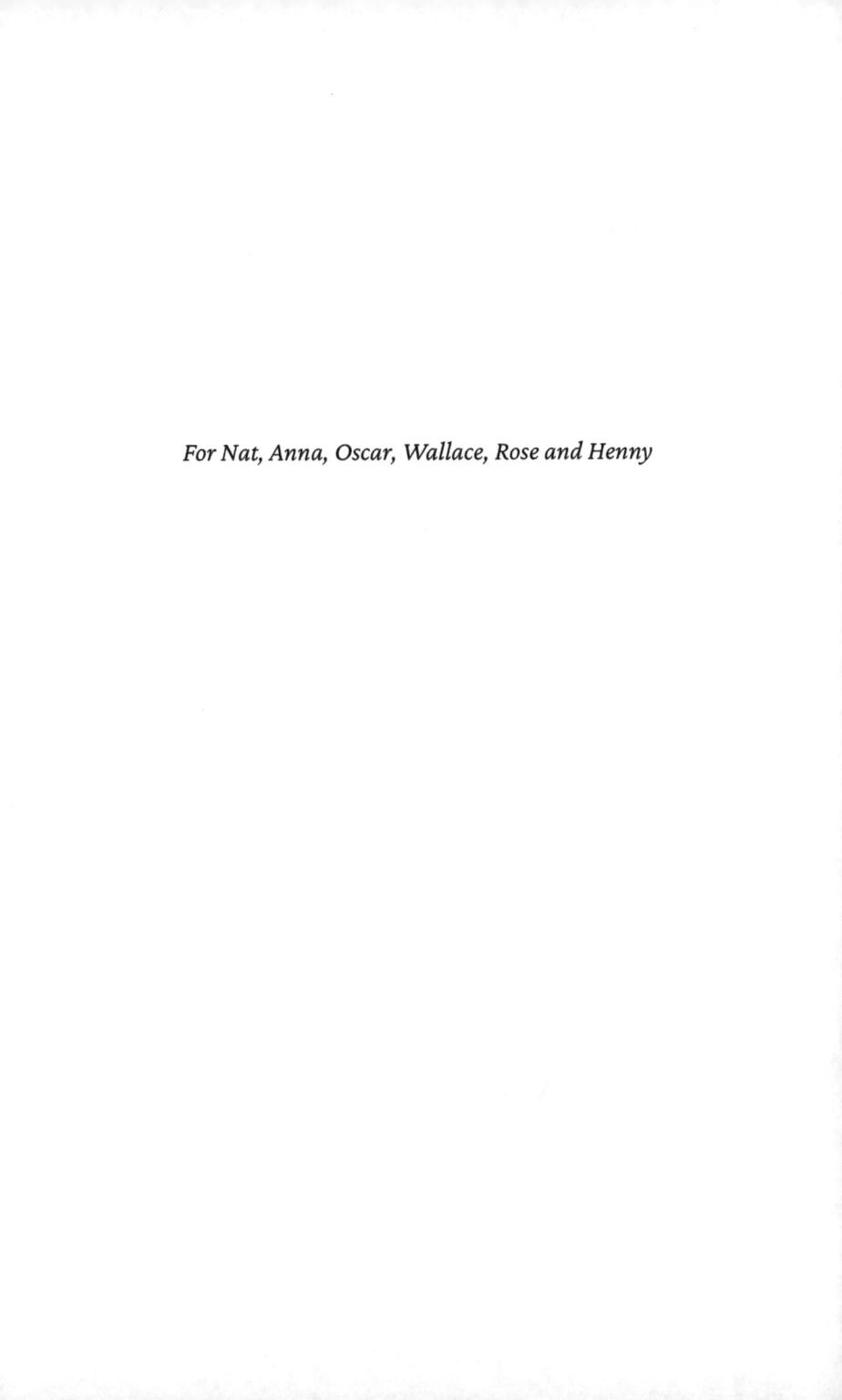

For Nat, Anna, Oscar, Wallace, Rose and Henny

PREFACE

One inspiration for this novel was the painting *The Girl I Left Behind Me* by Eastman Johnson. It is often on display at the Smithsonian Institution.

ONE

It was only two nights before Christmas and our houseboat was sinking, tipping into the dark waters of the lake. At first, I thought it was a bad dream. Flipping over, I pressed my cheek to my pillow and snuggled down under the blankets. Then a loud bang rattled me awake again. My eyes blinked open, and I caught a glimpse of my snow-globe with its miniature Space Needle glimmering on the nightstand. Another whistling pop sounded, and I sat up. Through the half-open door, I could see my mom wrapped in white twinkle lights, screaming, "Help, help me, I'm going to be electrocuted!"

What was Mom talking about? She looked crazy. Her short auburn hair, streaked green for Christmas, stuck out in all directions. Her red sequined dress glittered in the flickering lights, and she appeared to be standing ankle deep in water. At another time, I might have laughed. I did not laugh now. Mom was standing next to a hole where her stash of fireworks once sat. Water bubbled up from the floor. It occurred to me Mom never bought safe and sane fireworks. She preferred the more dangerous, illegal type. Now it looked like she had blown up our houseboat and quite possibly our lives.

Mom's boyfriend Del started untangling the lights. "No danger of being electrocuted, Celia. The lights run on batteries." Then he yelled, "Get up, Borgia. We're sinking." Moments later he stormed into my room, swooped me up from my nest of blankets and snapped, "Wake up, kid, we gotta get out of here pronto."

"Let me go, let me go," I yelled, pummeling him with both fists. "I'm not a baby." My mind was speeding. If we were moving again, I needed to pack.

I was pretty independent for a kid. Who knew how old I really was? As far as I knew there was no birth certificate to support any particular age. Mom had a friend help with the home delivery, so no official birth record seemed to exist. Mom didn't believe in filling out paperwork or even celebrating birthdays.

I was home schooled, if you can call it that. I got to choose my subjects, and most recently I had studied breeds of dogs and horses. I learned about the world by choosing favorite countries. At the moment, I was studying Italy. I had a huge picture of the leaning tower of Pisa pinned on my bedroom door. I found the poster in a pile of free stuff on the street where Mom and I liked to walk. Besides Italy, I had also studied Morocco, Tanzania and Spain. I focused on countries where the sun shines a lot. I knew enough about damp places, since my hometown sits smack in the middle of a rain forest. Yes, it rains a bunch in Seattle. Often it pours.

I knew a fast exit meant I would lose something in the chaos, a stuffed animal, my ruby slippers. Del piled my blankets back over me and tossed my purple rain boots on the bedspread. Even in my sleepy haze, I smiled. Nothing seemed to ruffle Del. Everything seemed to upset Mom.

I pulled on my rain boots, then my rather tattered Esmeralda costume with the coins that jingled in the pocket, finally my red parka with the fake-fur hood. Next I stepped into the rising water, grabbed my snow globe and shook it once until the silvery sparkles started drifting down on the golden Space Needle.

Finally, I packed three of my favorite books, nine of my naked Barbies, my blue nail polish and my cotton candy hand-lotion, stuffing everything into an old cello case that substituted for my suitcase. Next I dumped in my underwear drawer, added my favorite tee-shirts and worked on filling Mom's wicker case with the catch that had to be wired shut. I made sure I had both swimsuits, the blue one with orange polka dots and the pink one with green palm trees. Carefully, I wrapped my snow globe in a swimsuit, then stashed in a couple more naked Barbies and to be fair to them stuffed in a few of their crumpled outfits. I hated dressing Barbies. I did not play much with dolls anymore, so the gals usually went "commando," one of Del's favorite words.

"Stark naked is more like it," Mom always countered. "Borgia, put some clothes on those dolls right now." She hated stepping on any Barbie, whether clothed or not.

"Borgia! We're leaving in five," Mom yelled. She had a fierce grip on some black garbage bags and was sporting a felt hat tipped at a jaunty angle. A blue jay feather plucked off the sidewalk was stuck in the brim. Del reappeared, clad in several layers of clothing, including his cracked leather jacket and Sierra Club backpack. Two guitars were slung over his shoulder. Del didn't actually live with us, so I knew he wasn't leaving much behind like we were. It didn't seem fair.

"Back in a minute," Del yelled, grabbing my cello case. I waited on the edge of my bed, staring out the window, admiring the glowing lights of Seattle. Every few minutes, a boat decorated for Christmas glided by. I peeked over the edge of my covers. The water was still rising. It made my bed seem like a boat. At least I had my swimsuits. Best of all, I had carefully wrapped up the snow-globe that played the raindrops song when you wound the key. I noticed my pillowcase had dark streaks. I ran my fingers through my shoulder length hair. Mom had let me spray my hair any color I wanted for Christmas. She seemed genuinely surprised when I chose black.

"Because of Esmeralda?" she asked, as we stood in the drugstore examining boxes of temporary hair dye.

"Yep." I handed her a box featuring a raven-haired woman with long flowing tresses. For years I had obsessed over Esmeralda, a character from *The Hunchback of Notre Dame*. Esmerelda definitely did not have straw-colored hair like mine. Unfortunately, quite a bit of the dark hair dye had transferred to my pillowcase. Staring at the black streaks and the rising water all around me, I felt sad that we had to leave. This was our best rental ever, a floating houseboat smack in the heart of Seattle. A lump rose in my throat, and a numb tightness pulled at my stomach. "Do not cry," I told myself, but I felt as blurry and ruined as my stained pillowcase. "Stay calm, Borgia," I said out loud. Setting my jaw, I got up and waded out to where Mom and Del were frantically throwing clothes into garbage bags.

"You're one tough little girl," Del had told me numerous times. I knew I had to be really tough now.

Within minutes, we were trudging down the wooden pier, loaded down with bags and musical instruments, careful not to slip on the wet planks. Most of the houseboats were shrouded in shadows. Mom still had twinkle lights wrapped around her body, but she had switched them off so as not to draw attention. As I followed Mom and Del, I could see the giant Space Needle towering overhead, reaching high in the sky. Arrows of colorful light leapt up the sides, and way, way up at the tip top of the tower was a round flying saucer building where there used to be a really cool restaurant. Once, Mom and I rode the elevator all the way up and sat at a table with a white cloth. Mom ordered a dessert called Seattle Fog served on a tray shrouded in mist, just like a rainy Seattle day. All the time we were sharing spoonfuls of vanilla ice cream smothered in chocolate sauce, our table revolved in a circle, giving us a panoramic view of the city: ferryboats, snow-covered Mt. Rainier, the jagged mountain range to the east, even our houseboat huddled up against the shore like a miniature doll house.

I paused for a moment and glanced back at our houseboat one last time. It was definitely tipping. Even on the calmest day, the little house would rock when a wave hit, but nothing like this. If only we could still be curled up on the deck in our red chairs, listening to the water, hearing the slap, slap on the side of the houseboat.

"Keep up with us, Borgia." Del glanced back at me in the eerie dark. "Everything will be OK, don't worry." Del smiled. He always knew how to make me feel better.

"What about me?" Mom said. "I could have blown up back there." My stomach hurt just listening to her.

"What happened?" I asked, setting down my wicker case and beginning to drag it over the wet planks. We were passing rows of moored boats that looked like they were sleeping. I felt sorry for these boats tied to the dock. It was the holidays. They needed to be decorated with lights, gliding out over the water in the Christmas parade with all the other party ships.

"Don't ask," Mom said crossly. "Where do we go now?"

"Try not to worry," Del said. "We have the Jingle Bell Ball tomorrow night. That should be our focus. We can still make music."

"The sinking houseboat is my focus." Mom sniped in her harsh voice.

"Why on earth smoke cigarettes near fireworks, Celia?" Del's voice cracked with exasperation. Del did not smoke. He wanted Mom to quit. He told her cigarettes would ruin her voice. "Fireworks do not belong on a houseboat, especially illegal ones." Del sounded angry too. I could count on one hand the number of times Del challenged Mom directly. Yikes.

"It's not my fault," Mom said, turning to face him. "Fireworks left outside would be ruined by the rain. Duh?"

"Now the houseboat is ruined." I was impressed that Del stood his ground.

"No, we're ruined." Mom's voice rose to a high pitch. It all sounded bad. I shivered. It was starting to drizzle. A fine mist bathed my face. I pulled my hood tighter and made sure the zipper was all the way up.

"Mom, you should stop smoking," I said, softly. It bugged me that Mom puffed so many cigarettes. Del had showed me illustrations on the internet of smoke-damaged lungs. Mom said smoking kept her weight down. Unfortunately, now the emergency sirens were so loud, they blotted out my voice. Del and Mom glanced at each other as we passed under a dock light. They both looked worried. I was glad we were out of sight of the houseboat, away from the firetrucks and any police that might be arriving.

"Police won't look for us here," Mom said. "We are lucky it's so dark."

"No one home," Del nodded towards a houseboat with zero lights and a gloomy deck full of tangled, overturned chairs.

"Keith and Lana are in Palm Desert for Christmas," Mom reminded him as we huddled on their dock, surrounded by bags and instrument cases. I wished plastic Barbie arms and legs were not protruding from the edge of my wicker case. Mom got busy stashing the giant garbage bags on our neighbor's deck. She said we would pick them up later. When she was done, we walked down to the furthest edge of the dock, close to the main waterway and watched the Christmas boats gliding effortlessly over the water. Del pointed at a pool of light in the sky, eerie red and blue flashing lights in the direction of our houseboat.

"Maybe the police will stop the houseboat from sinking," I chirped hopefully. "Did you call 911?" Neither Mom nor Del answered. I took that as a no. "Maybe a neighbor heard the fireworks' explosion and will help." Still no response. It bugged me how adults don't feel like they have to answer a kid.

A huge white boat sailed into view, moving right by us at the end of the dock. Del held up his thumb like a hitchhiker.

"Turn on your lights, Celia. Maybe this yacht will give us a lift." Mom took off her crazy beret, fluffed her green Christmas hair. Soon she was blinking red and white again. She waved and smiled, even performed a little glittery dance while Del strummed on his guitar. I tried to stay out of sight, huddled in the shadows.

"Gigantic ship," I muttered.

"It's a yacht, Borgia," Del was looking at the boat, not at me. "Doesn't get much fancier, eh?" Del was from Canada. He often added "eh" at the end of his sentences.

"Hey," a man in a tuxedo called from the prow of the gleaming boat. It was by far the biggest Christmas ship I had ever seen. The man leaned over and aimed his long-stemmed glass at Del. "I recognize you. Guitarist from the band Tide's Out." Del saluted and nodded. "Know any Christmas music?" the man asked.

"Right O," Del said. "We do Hanukkah, too." Del sounded so cheerful. His shoulder length blond hair made him look like a rock star. Mom said Del was so handsome he could charm a snake. The yacht glided to a stop and a crew member threw Del a rope. Then he jumped onto the pier and wrapped the thick cord around a pylon and told us we could board. With one swift move, Del handed me up to a man in a black and white tuxedo.

Another man grabbed my cello case, and a lady wrapped in a white fur took the wicker one.

"That's my luggage," I said as a clutch of elegantly dressed people gathered around me and stared. These adults looked rich. Diamonds sparkled on wrists. Their clothes shone bright and new, not like our secondhand Value Village wardrobe.

"I can tell that suitcase belongs to you," a lady said, taking a sip from a pink drink. "I recognize a Barbie leg when I see one. I played with Barbie too back when I was a kid. I had no idea she would survive into the AI age."

Everyone peered down at the wicker case and the protruding legs and arms. The adults all held their glasses carefully, as if trying not to spill while the boat rocked gently. I thought they looked tipsy, like mom got after she took her pain pills. A blonde-haired lady in a black silk dress held on to the railing and giggled each time the boat tipped.

"I'm tired," I said, pulling on Del's leather jacket. All these people gawking at me made me feel strange. A beautiful woman in a sea-green gown with a diamond tiara in her hair reached down and took my hand.

"Are you a real princess?" I asked, gazing up at her in awe. She smiled.

"Paul thinks so." She handed me the bright red cherry in her drink. "I know a place where you can nap. I might take one, too." She led me away as I popped the cherry into my mouth. I glanced back at Mom and Del, who were taking sips from long stemmed glasses. Mom smiled at me and waved.

"It's OK," Del yelled. "I'll check on you in a few minutes, Borgia."

The princess lady led me down some highly polished wood stairs with gleaming brass railings. Through an open door, I glimpsed a bed with a golden coverlet and white feather pillows shaped like swans. Two round windows at the head of the bed twinkled with the lights of the city and their shimmering reflections on the dark water. Up on deck, Mom was singing "Santa Baby." Del accompanied her on guitar. Soon other voices joined in. Somebody was playing a piano.

The princess in the sea-green gown pulled the golden coverlet back and helped me up on the bed, propping a swan pillow under my head. I was so sleepy. The lull of the boat and the music rocked me gently. The princess lady sank down in a rose-colored chair, its white arms carved like the necks of swans.

"I'm going to close my eyes for just a moment," she said in a dreamy voice. "Parties make me so sleepy."

"What fairy tale princess are you?" I asked. The lady was beautiful.

"Hmmm, I don't know. Which one do you think?"

"Sleeping Beauty," I said, "only with dark hair. Maybe Snow White since she had black hair."

"Like yours." She gave me a sleepy half smile. I touched my hair. I forgot about my black hair dye. I took the white pillow from under my head and spread the hood of my coat out flat, so I wouldn't get dark streaks on the lovely white swan. "How about you?" the lady asked. "What princess are you?"

"I'm not a princess. I like the Esmeralda character though." I opened my coat and showed her my costume, Mom had found in a thrift store. I did not tell her my hair was only sprayed black, that my real hair was the color of straw.

"Why did you choose a poor girl like Esmeralda instead of a princess?" She looked perplexed. I knew exactly why, but I would only tell her part of the answer.

"I like the coins that jingle," I said. That was true. My Esmeralda costume was decorated with golden coins. What I did not say was that Mom and Del never had any money. When they got money, they spent it. I loved the idea of having coins in my pocket all the time or sewn on my costume like this. I knew this lady with her diamond bracelet and fancy clothes must have plenty of money. Even though I was a kid, I knew Mom was different from our houseboat neighbors. Mom moved often. I didn't want to talk about it. My costume was ragged, a couple years old and getting too small for me, but I still loved it.

"Oh," the princess lady said, studying the golden coins attached to my skirt. She suddenly got up and placed her diamond tiara on my head. "You are the real princess. I crown you Princess Esmeralda, my gift to you." I blinked and closed my eyes. "Wait, don't fall asleep yet. What's your name?"

"Borgia," I mumbled. My eyelids felt heavy like rocks were weighing them down.

"Borgia what?"

"OftheGlades."

"Strange last name," the lady wrinkled her forehead. "Suits a princess, though. Princess Borgia. Borgia OftheGlades." A dreamy half smile lit up her face and she sank back down in the chair and closed her eyes.

The crown on my head felt too heavy and pointy. I didn't want to be rude, but I couldn't wear a crown while I slept. I pulled it off and stashed it in my wicker suitcase. Then I lay back down, making sure my parka was still protecting the pillows from my black hair dye. In a moment, I fell fast asleep.

TWO

"Wake up Borgia. Mannie brought his car to pick us up." I rubbed my eyes. Was this a dream? I was definitely under a golden coverlet with white swan pillows at my side. Instead of the princess lady in a sea-green dress, Mom was perched on the edge of the rose armchair, brushing her teeth and spitting into a glass of water. Del stood at the end of the bed latching my suitcase. He handed me my purple rain boots. Soon I followed Mom and Del up the stairs, holding on to the shining brass railing.

When I stepped onto the dock, I could see Mannie across the street, his hands folded deep in the pockets of his long trench coat. He was leaning against his crazy black car that used to be a hearse, a car that hauls dead bodies. Mom called his car the Coffin. Now, everybody called it the Coffin. Mannie was in Del's band. He never said much, but he could really play the drums. Now he bowed and opened the car door, ushering me into the back seat.

"I need a bathroom," I said to Mom as the car pulled out of the parking space. Mom took a long puff on her cigarette and looked at me in the rearview mirror.

"Hold tight, we are stopping real soon."

"Did the houseboat really sink?" The car was speeding uphill, away from the water.

"Who knows? That old houseboat was half rotten." Mom glared at me in the mirror. "Not our fault," she said, tapping her cigarette ashes into a tray between the seats.

"Kind of our fault," Del said, sitting next to me. "Fireworks should burst over the water, not inside the living room." Then he whispered in my ear. "Just say no to smoking." I nodded and stared at the Christmas trees in people's front windows and all the crazy decorations outside on the lawns. My favorite was a white mesh reindeer with antlers wrapped in blue lights, still lit during the day. Most of the blowup decorations of Santas and snow men lay flat and deflated.

"Fireworks in the house?" Mannie's measured voice sounded puzzled as he spun the steering wheel while we rounded a corner. There was a pregnant pause, so he added, "It's Christmas, right, not Fourth of July?" His long black hair protruding from under the rim of his broad brimmed hat was the only view I had of him from the back seat.

Del didn't say anything, but Mom piped up. "In a few days it's a new year. People celebrate, set off fireworks on New Year's Eve." The sharp edge to her voice made me nervous.

That comment shut Mannie up too. The Coffin continued to strain uphill, away from the lake, away from all the houseboats clinging to the shoreline. The sky was a dark sheet of grey with iron tinted clouds. Rivulets of water ran along the road and into the storm drains.

"I doubt the houseboat sank," Mom said, thinking out loud. "All those sirens and lights. I'm sure the fire department dealt with it. Not our problem, thank God."

"And we got paid this week," Del said cheerfully. He

sounded like himself again. "A stop at Dick's Drive-in, Mannie? Hey Borgia, want some French fries?"

"I want to find a restroom." I kicked off my purple rain boots, then reached down and cracked the lid of my wicker suitcase. My snow globe glimmered back at me, still half wrapped in a swimsuit, surrounded by naked Barbies and the beautiful princess crown studded with diamonds. It sparkled happily.

"Oh no, I left my blue sneakers in the houseboat." My ruby slippers had left glitter all over the Barbies and my underwear, so I pulled them out and tucked the purple boots on top of the princess crown.

"Shoes are the least of your worries, Borgia. There's the restroom. Be quick." Mom pointed to a battered metal door on the side of a gas station. Mannie had turned into a parking space marked "Handicapped Only." I stepped out, right into an oil spattered puddle.

I never liked public restrooms. In this particular one, the metal door didn't latch. I couldn't reach the paper towels. The green soap dispenser was empty, and only the cold water worked. The mirror was murky and smeared with the word "punk face" in red lipstick. Still, I felt a hundred percent better when I came out. My fries were ready. I even got my own fry sauce. It tasted way better than ketchup.

"No gluten in fries," Mom was saying. She no longer ate gluten or dairy, so I guess I wasn't either. "You'll be OK with potatoes. They are healthy. God knows you can stand a little fat in your diet, you skinny kid." Mom was always talking about health food. What she could eat, what she couldn't. I found it all boring. I focused on not dropping fries on the seat as we headed out in bumper-to-bumper traffic down busy Lake City Way. Mom and Del were trying to decide what to do with me during the concert. Ordinarily I could stay home alone—not an option now the houseboat was sinking.

"Does Volly still babysit?" Mannie asked, trying to be helpful.

"No," I screamed, "not Volly." I reached down and unclipped my seatbelt. I could not stand Volly.

"I agree. Not Volly," Del said, calmly putting his arm around me. He helped me click my seatbelt back into place.

"The Crocodile Concert Hall is so strict about children," Mom mused. "The police threatened to call Child Protective Services if Borgia ever appears at our concert again."

"Because they serve alcohol," Mannie said. "A state law. No children at concerts that serve alcoholic beverages."

"Stupid," Mom said.

"Mom, can I hide in the concert hall cupboards like I did when I was little? I'll be quiet as a mouse." I ran my fingers over my lips, zipped them closed. "The police don't know about my hiding space." I was desperate not to be left with some weird babysitter like Volly. I never wanted to be left at her house again.

"Maybe," Mom said. "Volly may be our only option." A deathly silence settled over the car, and I began kicking the back of Mom's seat. "Stop it, Borgia." I quit, but the tension still hung in the air. Then Mom relented. " I guess it's our only option. Concert cupboards one last time. Jingle Bell Ball, Crocodile Hall, for you, Borgia," she chirped in an almost happy voice.

I exhaled with relief, and my breath fogged up the passenger window. I felt so joyful, I drew a happy face on the steamy glass.

"Where we headed? Hurrah, I get to go to the concert." I poked Del in the side. He grinned. I felt so happy, I wanted to hang my head out the window like a dog. It felt like the sun had just come out from behind a cloud, but in reality, Mannie was turning on the windshield wipers. "Is that snow," I yelled, "just in time for Christmas?"

"Terrible," Mannie muttered.

Minutes later, we pulled into a dingy parking garage to pick up Lionel. Lionel was the lead guitar player in Del's band. He usually looked worried and angry. His brow was furrowed like a bulldog's, and his thick neck was covered with Frankenstein nail tattoos. Mom said he was just a big baby and not to be afraid of him. He liked to toss me around like a scary carnival ride. Sometimes I enjoyed it, but generally, it made me anxious. I pressed my cheek against the cold window and blotted out my steamy, happy face.

We sped downhill back to the Seattle waterfront and dropped off the band instruments at the Crocodile Concert Hall. After a brief commotion, everybody piled back in the car. I sat next to Dell, glad that Lionel was on the other side. I looked down at the Coffin's padded sides with the rips puffing out like a cotton dispenser. I liked riding in this old funeral car, even if it had been used to haul dead bodies. It was long and sleek, with tons of room in the cushioned area, so safe for our fragile band instruments—even perfect for musicians who needed to stretch out and take a nap.

Mannie steered the car along the winding waterfront through Golden Gardens Park. Only a few folks appeared on the beach, braced against the snowy wind, shrouded in hooded parkas. Most were walking dogs in the drizzle. Happy to be in the car, I watched the windshield wipers churn out a pleasant rhythm, while big wet flakes pelted the glass.

"A beaver dam," Mannie exclaimed. "Look at the big pile of sticks near the edge of that pond."

"Gadzooks!" Lionel exclaimed. "Look how a beaver has been gnawing on those trees."

"Cool," I added as I studied the rows of tooth marks on a row of skinny Alder trees.

"Not cool," Mom countered. Manny began to hum to himself, ignoring our comments. Hard to know what he was thinking.

CHAPTER

THREE

Minutes later, we skidded into an asphalt parking lot overlooking Puget Sound. Grey Seagulls with pink legs rose in the ocean breeze a few feet off the pavement and immediately set back down, tucking their wings to their side. Beady eyes glared at me. The birds looked cold and hungry. I managed to throw a few fries in their direction and create a crazy flapping and squawking, as they fought over my scraps. Walking backward against the wind, I stopped for a moment at the bottom of the corrugated steps to throw the very last fry.

Mom tweaked the back of my head.

" Mom," I yelled, and swatted her hand away.

"Keep walking," she said and plunged ahead of me up the stairs to the restaurant. I followed, rubbing my head and paused mesmerized in front of green fir boughs wrapped round the knotted beams in the entrance. Bronze salmon, wearing red Santa hats, leapt over a huge wreath with a droopy bow that adorned the fireplace mantle. I rubbed my hands together in front of the gas fire, while everyone tumbled coats and scarves onto the backs of chairs and squeezed in around crowded tables. Each time the door opened, a rush of cold sea air whooshed into the dining room, mingling with the fragrance of fresh sea food.

I found a perfect spot and kneeled down on the floor next to a giant picture window sprayed with droplets of rain. Grey Puget Sound spread out before me. A few brave boats bobbed on the choppy waves, along with diving ducks.

"What you looking at?" Del paused behind me as I leaned my face against the cold glass.

"Nothing," I said.

"See that black and white duck?" I looked, and all of a sudden, the duck disappeared. "Keep watching. It's not really gone." Moments later, the duck popped back up to the surface.

"Is that a fish in its beak?"

" Yep." Del laughed and continued to stare out the window with me. " Look over there. Way up on top of the sailboat mast is a sassy bird called a King Fisher." I followed Del's finger to the high mast of a boat wedged among many other crafts in their moorings. The tiny bird was blue and white with a jagged top notch like a crazy buzzcut.

"Maybe I'll study birds next," I said, but Del had already turned away and was talking to Lionel.

"Come sit here beside me, Borgia." Mom rattled the ice in her drink at me and patted the chair next to her, but I was so captivated by the diving ducks, I stayed put. Across the inlet, not far from the restaurant, a high cliff rose on the shore. The raw cliff edge was fringed at the top with haphazard bushes, half their roots exposed.

While I sat on the carpet, the conversation clattered around me. I could see Mom's foot tapping nervously under the table, and Del patting her knee supportively. She had twisted her napkin into a tight knot and made a triangle out of her straw. Both had fallen on the floor. When a cup of hot chocolate with whipped cream and sprinkles arrived, I finally joined the others and slipped into the chair next to Mom. The waiter smiled and handed me a snowman cookie decorated with a red frosting scarf and a blacktop hat.

"What would you like to order?" he asked me.

"Fish and chips, but no coleslaw." I gave him a big smile.

"Borgia!" Mom raised her eyebrows and glared at me across the table

"OK, a little coleslaw." I was enjoying sourdough bread with melted butter, happy Mom was not making me stay gluten free on Christmas Eve.

I knew Mom wanted me to eat more vegetables, but I was excited when the fish and chips arrived. Glancing around the table, I noted Mom poking at crab legs and Del devouring a slab of salmon. Mannie picked at a shrimp cocktail, while Lionel cut into a giant steak.

Festive music and laughter floated on the air. After our meal, we pushed back in our chairs and relaxed. Del tipped a toothpick back and forth in his mouth, while Mom and I sucked on red and white peppermints.

"Look," Mom said, as the twilight sky started to fade to black. She pointed to the cliff house, now glowing with lights.

"Like a castle," I added.

"Is it possible Marley is home?" Mom asked. Marley was one of Del's wealthy musician friends. He owned the cliff house but was rarely in residence. A fence tipped drunkenly all along the edge of the property.

Del leaned over and explained that over many years erosion was the reason bushes and trees were falling onto the beach. The trees at the cliff's edge, tipped at crooked angles, their scraggly roots exposed. Some trees had already tumbled down, then been lashed by the waves.

"Let's check on Marley," Mom said, staring at the house,

and minutes later we were back in the coffin, heading up the steep, winding streets, through neighborhoods where mansions with perfect lawns opened to amazing views of Puget Sound. I zeroed in on a green and white ferry boat way below, that looked like a toy boat floating in a bathtub.

"These houses are all about the views," Mannie said, as if talking to himself.

"All about money you mean," Mom added, peering out the window.

Moments later, we arrived at the spectacular house, down a long winding drive lined by a wild leafy hedge that looked like it needed a trim. I tumbled out of the car and ran toward the dangerous cliff, hoping to see our restaurant, maybe even the window where I looked at birds. The jagged weather-beaten fence, leaning on its drunken posts, looked much larger than it did from the restaurant window.

"Borgia!" Del yelled in a frantic voice. "Stop. The ground is unstable." He ran after me, grabbed the hood of my parka and yanked me to an abrupt halt. I spun around and swatted at his hand, clenching my teeth against the bracing wind. My cheeks stung. My red coat flapped open like a cape, but I knew Del meant well, so I settled down and walked back toward the house, holding his hand, noting how each of our steps left soggy footprints in the grass. We followed a winding stone path that passed through an ornate cast iron gate leading to a patio with a big fire pit.

Through the glass slider, I could see a crowded music studio full of cords and microphones and guitars. Mannie sat high on a platform, pounding away on a drum set. Del soon left me to join the other musicians, and Mom motioned to me from the sofa where she was folded up in a corner. She offered me a sip of her coke, and I wedged myself in some giant pillows next to her and watched the musicians adjust their instruments.

"Celia, I got us a gig!" Del jumped in front of us, strumming a celebratory chord on his guitar. "Guess where?"

"No clue," Mom tipped her head back and took a swig of cola.

"Paris!" Del crowed, his eyes glowing. "France, Celia. We open for Marley. He said he will pay for plane tickets, you and me. Plus we stay in his apartment for free." He enunciated the next sentences carefully through his teeth, half whispering, but I heard him just fine. "Marley said no kids. We need to find a place for Borgia." I could see Marley in his blue jeans and beaded moccasins cross the room, a big grin on his face. He lifted a bottle aloft as if to offer a toast.

"I'm coming too," I yelled. "You can't leave me behind."

"Shh, Del, think before you speak," Mom tried to hand me her can of cola, but I pushed it away. Del shrugged, turned and walked off, continuing to strum cheerful chords. Mom wrapped her arms around me. "Don't worry kiddo. Have I ever left you behind?"

I didn't answer. I knew it would make Mom mad, but yes, yes, she had left me behind. I wanted to trust her. I felt safe with Del, but this Paris talk made me uneasy. France was really far away.

I leaned closer to Mom on the sofa. Somehow, the whole cliff house experience creeped me out. Del said one day the house would fall into Puget Sound. The idea of being left behind while Mom and Del went to Paris seemed almost like falling off a cliff. I did not want to end up in the cold, cold water of Puget Sound like the cliff house or our house boat.

CHAPTER

FOUR

When the Coffin finally pulled into the alley back of the Crocodile Concert Hall, I was extremely tired. I trudged past the garbage cans where a couple of homeless folks leaned against the brick building, curled up under grungy blankets. Then I climbed the concrete steps, each one making me feel more weary.

When Del pulled open the metal door to the concert hall, I felt an electric surge of happiness. For some reason, this old concert building, only blocks from the Seattle Waterfront, always sparked fond memories. I was reminded of Mom playing her accordion. I pictured the dark blue velvet lining of her battered leather case. When I was little, I liked to cram myself up next to the velvet, curl up like a kitten, while Mom pushed the black and white buttons and keys making great music.

When she was a little girl, Mom took accordion lessons from an Italian man. "Frank was so handsome, big brown eyes, dark wavy hair," Mom's voice sounded dreamy whenever she talked about her teacher. I had heard the stories a million times. The memories sprang open the moment I stepped foot inside the halls of the old building. Maybe the funky smell reminded me of Mom's battered leather case. At any rate I was full of life again. I ran down the hall to our usual waiting room, where performers holed up until it was their turn on stage.

These waiting rooms were dingy and rundown, but I didn't mind. No one had painted the place in ages, and cracks zigged and zagged over the floor. I had to be careful not to trip on the loose tiles. A row of splintered cupboards ran along the wall—storage space for an assortment of odds and ends—microphones, cords, clothes, anything performers wanted to stash while on stage. Years ago, I had crawled inside one of these cupboards and fashioned a makeshift bed out of a pile of coats. I wrapped my Barbies in scarves and set out some of my favorite candy in a Dixie cup. I had my own fort, cozy and safe. By keeping quiet and not complaining, I no longer had to stay with weird babysitters like Volly. Perfect. Mom and Del were close by, even when performing on stage. Unfortunately, a couple times, the security guard caught me wandering in the hall and had warned Mom, "no children allowed in the concert hall tonight." Mom said I had to stay hidden the whole time, or I might be put in foster care. That meant living with strangers. Yikes! Not happening.

Not long after we arrived, Mannie's girlfriend, Harlo showed up to help him set up the drums. Her short black hair was bobbed with purple highlights. Tonight she wore dangly earrings and two nose rings. I always counted the holes in her tights—six big ones, two little, plus a short black skirt and unlaced hiking boots. "Harlo is dramatic," Mom told me. "She's an artist."

While Harlo worked on the drum set, Lionel unloaded his guitar, then paced back and forth in the waiting room like a caged tiger. Lionel was always a nervous wreck before a concert. Unfortunately, as I walked by him, he picked me up and tossed me over his shoulder like a sack of potatoes. Soon I was flying through the air on one of his unfortunate human carnival rides.

"Hey kiddo, cast a spell with those ruby slippers, OK? I need good vibes tonight."

"Put me down first," I pleaded. Lionel set me down a bit roughly, and I hopped across the room, shaking a pair of jingle bells I had found on the floor. "Before I cast a spell, you need to play a song from *The Wizard of Oz*," I said glancing at him over my shoulder.

"Lionel started to strum his guitar and sing, "Somewhere over the rainbow blue birds sing,"

"The words are 'bluebirds fly' not 'sing,'" I corrected him.

"Give me a break, kid." Lionel shook his head and furrowed his brow. "I don't sing rainbow songs every day, OK? How about that spell with the ruby slippers?"

I nodded, scrunched my nose, closed my eyes and clicked my ruby slippers together three times just like in the movie. "I wish we could all go home right now," I said, picturing the houseboat.

"Not home," Lionel protested. "I spent my whole life trying to get away from that dump."

He grabbed me under my arms and spun me around three more times. "Home is where your heart is," he snapped. "Music is my home."

Lionel had crazy tattoos all up and down his muscular arms. The wild scenes kind of scared me, because there were red eyed devils riding motorcycles and black skulls with snakes curling out of the eye sockets. He was generally a friendly guy, so I closed my eyes and didn't look at his tattoos. Mom said Lionel was often agitated because he had low self-esteem, but she said he could really play the guitar, even better than Del.

"It's a bigger crowd than we expected, considering it's Christmas Eve," Mom said, stepping out from behind one of the dressing room screens. She held a mascara wand in one hand and a can of hair spray in the other. Sinking down in a metal folding chair, she started gluing on false eyelashes.

Lionel finally set me down, "There's like zero stagehands," Lionel said. "We gotta do everything ourselves. Hey, where's Mannie?"

"Getting some fresh air," Harlo answered, as she lay out Mannie's numerous drumsticks in a neat row on the counter.

"He's late." Lionel pulled his guitar strap over his shoulder.

"Mannie never lets us down," Del said authoritatively, as he stepped through the doorway. "He picked us up in the Coffin today, saved our hides after the houseboat fiasco."

Mom pointed her mascara wand at me. "Borgia, we'll be on stage soon. Do you have my phone?" I held it up. "Silence the ringer. No calls. Del will text you if you need to hide, or if you need to contact me."

"I know the drill," I slipped the phone into my pocket. This was our routine. Sometimes Mom texted me if I needed to disappear. She never got tired of telling me we could all be arrested if I broke the rules.

"Do you have a spot picked out?" Mom was still looking at herself in the mirror, fooling around with the green spikes in her hair.

I nodded, twirled over to a cupboard and flipped open the door. My suitcase was stashed among all the coats, along with Mom's purse and a pile of her clothes. My cello case was leaning against the first cupboard. I smiled to myself as I remembered a secret about the cupboards. I hadn't shared it with anybody, ever. I was not about to share it now.

"Five minutes until show time." A stage manager stuck his head through the door while tapping the keys on his iPad.

Mannie stepped into the room right behind him. "Ready everyone?" He picked up his drumsticks and gave Harlo a kiss.

The only time I saw Mannie smile was before a concert. Most of the time his face had the flat expression of a pancake.

"Ready," Del said. High fives were slapped all round. Mom ruffled my hair. Then the band was out the door and down the hall. Stoked by the excitement, the buzz from the crowd and the roars echoing when a favorite musician appeared on stage, I paused in anticipation. Sure enough, the applause hit, the electric storm of voices rose, and the music ratcheted up in volume.

Happy to be alone, I twirled round and round in the now empty room, then quietly slipped into the cupboards. I had hidden in these beat up enclosures at least twenty times and knew every shadowy space. I was eager to see if my secret spot still existed. Years ago, on the back wall of the middle cupboard, I had discovered a small sliding door that opened into a similar set of closed shelves off the main stage. The surrounding area was crowded with props, music stands, old speakers and a snarl of folding chairs, all layered with cobwebs and dust. From the shadows, you could glimpse the intriguing maze of ropes and pulleys that controlled the velvet curtains framing the main stage. Overhead was a starlike ceiling of lights and a narrow catwalk I dreamed about walking on someday when I was older.

Eagerly, I pushed on the secret door, thrilled as I managed to wedge it open. Shoving my red parka through the opening, I smoothed it out like a rug, pressing out all the lumps. Somehow, I managed to squeeze my wicker suitcase through too. From this spot, I could actually watch the bands perform. I could even sneak on stage, hide myself in the grand old curtains and catch a view of the writhing audience.

Tonight, the standing-room-only crowd was decked out in felt reindeer antlers, plush Santa hats and glowing red and green necklaces, some blue and white for Hanukkah. As I snuck on stage, I folded myself in a velvet curtain, searching the shadowy figures for children. Of course, there were none. Not allowed. Then I spied a lighted necklace, tossed onto center stage, only a few feet in front of me. The glowing red and green ring was so close, I wanted it. Only a few steps and it would be mine.

Music exploded all around me, as shadowy figures gyrated to the beat. No one would notice me, right? In a flash, I stepped in front of the curtains, made a mad dash and scooped up the necklace and pulled it over my head. Its red and green glow connected me to the audience. I paused to admire Mom, her mouth close to the microphone. In the bright spotlight, her voice crackled through the concert hall. Lionel jumped in the air, jerking his guitar up and down like a jack hammer. Del strode dramatically back and forth playing his guitar, sometimes joining Mom at the microphone. High up on his platform, Mannie pounded the drums, shaking his long hair. Mom's slim body moved rhythmically, and without hesitation I joined in too, dancing, swaying, with a piece of velvet curtain. I took a couple side twirls, completely caught up in the moment. No one would notice me when such bright lights were focused on my mom and her band.

By the time the band's set was over, I was spent. I slipped back into the cupboards, lay flat on my back, waiting for Mom and Del to signal me. Admiring the glow from my beautiful necklace, at some point I fell asleep. I dreamed that I stood at the microphone myself. Then I jerked awake as Mom's cell phone vibrated against my hip like an angry hornet. When my eyes adjusted to the bright light, I read her text message:

Borgia stay in the cupboards.

Don't say anything.

Be completely quiet.

The police are here.

CHAPTER

FIVE

ngry voices jangled in my ears. I edged back into the waiting room cupboard and peeked through a crack. Two policemen stood inches away, guns snug in holsters, their uniformed striped pants and thick black boots so close I could reach out and touch them.

"Is a child with you or not?" a policeman asked.

"No child," Mom said curtly. "I don't see a child."

"Nope," Del's voice agreed cheerfully. "It's against the law to bring a kid to a place where alcohol is served."

"Didn't stop you in the past," the officer snapped. "Tonight a kid was goofing around on stage during your performance."

Uh oh, the police saw me. I got Mom and Del in trouble. I frantically edged back into the secret cupboard and slid the door behind me just in time. I heard the first set of cupboard doors pop open and a rustling of coats.

"That's my purse," Mom said.

"Yeah, well are these your pills?" The officer's voice was sarcastic. "Do you have a prescription?"

"Just a bunch of clothes in here," another officer said, as the scuffling noises continued. "Wait, some dolls wrapped in scarves."

I held my breath, afraid I might cough from the dust. My throat tickled. More doors slammed. The cop voices sounded harsh, not like the smiling policeman who patrolled the dock near our houseboat. I could no longer make out what they were saying. Mom was yelling, arguing with one of them about her purse. I couldn't stand it. I rolled back into the original cupboards and peeked through the crack. My heart dropped. Mom was handing a card to Lionel, while a policeman clicked handcuffs on Del's wrists. Mom was cuffed next.

I heard her hiss, "Emergency plan. Give this card to Mannie, OK, Lionel?" I held my breath and clamped my hand over my mouth. My heart was pounding.

The policeman said, "You have the right to remain silent. You have the right to...." I lost the rest of his words.

"Nobody here stole any jewelry," Mom said irritably. There were more shuffling sounds, doors slammed. Then an eerie silence descended. Finally, Lionel spoke.

"What the hell," he said. "I can't take care of a kid."

"Lionel, follow the emergency plan," Mom's desperate voice sounded at a distance from the hallway.

"It's OK, Celia." Mannie's voice was there now, the calm voice of reason. "Don't worry, I've got this."

Lionel started throwing open the cupboards until he found me and dragged me out. He grabbed my cello case. I grabbed my wicker suitcase.

"We need to leave right now," he said. "Follow me." I felt sick. Mannie was gone. Lionel was in charge. This might be worse than being left with the babysitter, Volly. I followed him out the door into the back alley.

I could see the black hearse, hear its engine idling. Mannie and Harlo were sitting in the front seat.

"Get in kid." Lionel cracked the back door. Two homeless people, leaning against the brick wall, watched with interest. One of them held up a battered hat, hoping for some spare change. I hesitated, then slid into the back seat, next to my cello case. Lionel handed Mannie the card Mom had given him. Then he slammed the car door and turned away. I was relieved. Apparently, Lionel was not coming. His tattoos and thick neck were too scary without Mom, without Del, to make me feel safe.

Rummaging through my wicker suitcase, I found a package of Skittles underneath the princess crown the beautiful girl had given me. Opening a window, I prepared to drop bright colored pieces in the alley, like I had done when I made my escape from the dreaded babysitter Volly.

"Close the window, Borgia. It's freezing." Harlo shot me a nasty look. I shoved the candy into my coat pocket and leaned back against the seat. Snowflakes splatted the windshield. "Turn up the heat," Harlo demanded.

The woman wrapped in a blanket set her hat down but kept staring at us as we drove away. Where would she sleep tonight now that it was snowing? Where was I going to sleep? How do you sleep outdoors in the snow?

"Where are we going?" I demanded, as the glimmering lights of high-rise buildings towered over us as we sped through downtown Seattle toward the freeway.

"Who knows?" Mannie said. A few minutes later, we entered a long, lighted tunnel with walls of yellow tile. When we emerged, we were on the giant floating bridge that spanned Lake Washington. I stared at the choppy white-capped waves on one side of the bridge and the calm water on the other. Mom always criticized the Eastside communities across the lake. She said, "We will never, ever live in the suburbs, Borgia. Boring, boring, too much money, too many snobs."

I believed her. Mom would not send me across the lake,

send me out of the city to the land of boring snobs. My stomach started to ache.

"I don't want to leave Seattle," I said adamantly. "Drop me off at the houseboat. Maybe it didn't sink after all. I can wait for Mom there."

Harlo and Mannie were silent. I pulled Mom's cell phone out of my pocket and saw the battery icon was bright orange, practically dead. Now I couldn't even text. "Mom's cell phone battery died."

"Give it to me," Harlo said, extending her hand between the seats. "I can charge it." I set my mom's phone in the palm of her hand.

"Why did the police take Mom and Del? Was it because of me?"

"Doubt it," Mannie said.

"Big mystery," Harlo said, glancing back at me.

"Your mom will call as soon as she can." Mannie tried to reassure me as we exited off the bridge under a flash of blue lights.

"Dang, I forgot it's a toll bridge," Manny, cried out. "They just took a picture of my license. Rats!" The snow was coming down harder than ever, in big swirling flakes as the windshield wipers whipped back and forth, grinding on the glass. At least the sound was rhythmical actually comforting. Heat fogged up the windows, but I didn't feel like drawing any pictures.

The car struck out down another busy freeway, heading north. All the cars whizzed by, making me dizzy. Mom and Del almost never drove on the freeway. I gazed out the back window where the lights of Seattle still glimmered across the lake. Oh no, I thought, I am in the boring suburbs.

Mom's warning about too many rich people rang in my head. She also liked to complain there were a lot of wild animals–bears, coyotes, even cougars and bobcats.

"You just missed the exit," Harlo yelled.

"So what? I can get off at the next one." Mannie gripped the wheel, intently peering through the blinding flakes and the crazy high speed wipers.

"The snow is sticking," Harlo's voice crackled with anxiety.

"At least the cars are slowing down," Mannie added.

"Yeah, but we could get stuck in a traffic jam," Harlo sounded worried. "I'm glad we are getting off the freeway."

To my surprise, once we took the exit, houses and trees popped into view much like those in Seattle.

"We're taking our lives in our hands," Harlo complained as the car swerved onto an unplowed road several inches deep in powdery snow. "Where on earth is this place?"

Mannie didn't answer. At some point, the houses disappeared, replaced by pastures with horses huddled in sheds, many covered in belted blankets. They looked cold. Soon, tall fir trees penned us in on all sides. The narrow ribbon of white road coursed between them and an infrequent lonely streetlight. You could not see anything through the giant trees, no countryside, no houses. We were in a forest tunnel. When would it end? When would I see the bright city, the lake, the mountains? As the snow got deeper, the heavy branches loomed toward us, their boughs weighed down with ice. The road rose steeper and steeper, and the car wound up and around, occasionally veering crazily near the pillowy snowdrifts.

"Are you sure this is the right road?" Harlo asked, in a strangled voice.

"I'm not sure of anything right now," Manny snapped. Frustration had crept into his usually measured voice. "I've never been here, either."

It sounded like we were lost, so I cracked the back window again and began dropping candy, trying to leave a path, but the pieces disappeared.

"Close the window; it's freezing." Harlo glared at me in the rearview mirror. "Mannie, your navigation has gone crazy. This is a mountain road. " She sounded hysterical.

"Quit exaggerating," Mannie said quietly. "We're in the foothills." The road ahead split suddenly, and a triangular yellow sign with a black Y glowed in our headlights. "Left, or right?" Mannie turned to Harlo who peered at her cell phone.

"Can't tell. Doesn't say. Go right and keep moving. We'll never get traction again if we stop." Mannie veered right, and the tall trees and snow closed in upon us even more.

Only our headlights pierced the darkness, while the windshield wipers ground out a strangled rhythm, struggling to clear a view. After several miles, just when Mannie said he was going to turn back, an old-fashioned neon light appeared up ahead. The words "Dog Pound" were lit up in red, and under that, a blue sign in all caps said, FURRY FRIENDS ANIMAL SHELTER. Near the gate a lone light on a spindly pole illuminated the millions of snowflakes twirling down like tiny ballerinas. An ice encrusted chain link fence ran around a stucco building that seemed to be cobbled together with a modern structure in the back. It looked like a cross between a veterinarian clinic and a private home. Inside the fence, a mound of snow took the shape of a small car, the only vehicle in the circular drive.

The gate was closed, so Mannie pulled up next to the streetlight and put the car in park. Glancing around, I noticed several nondescript sheds in what appeared to be an open pasture. Across the road the forest rose up again like a huge wall.

"This has to be it," Mannie said, staring down at the card Mom handed Lionel just before the police took her away. He stepped out of the car into deep snow, then opened the Coffin's tailgate and set my cello and wicker suitcases against the chain link fence.

"Hey," I yelled. "What are you doing? This says animal shelter. It's a dog pound."

"You like dogs, Borgia," Mannie's voice sounded falsely sweet.

"Have you even been here before?" Harlo turned to me. She was no longer hysterical.

"No," I said adamantly. "Never! I don't want to be here."

"Let's just check it out," She flashed a tepid smile. "I bet your mom knows someone here. See that dog flip-flop in the front door? I think you're small enough to squeeze through it and report back to us."

I shook my head. I did not plan to stick my head through a weird dog flip-flop in a crazy animal shelter.

"Come on, Borgia. We just drove a million miles through a blizzard to do your mom's bidding. It's freezing out." Harlo pulled her purple scarf up higher on her neck, then crossed her arms and glared at me.

Mannie's black coat was now dusted with snow. His hands crammed in his coat pockets, he was walking along the tamped down tire tracks in the road, using his cell phone as a flashlight to illuminate the chain link fence.

"Lights are on in the back," he yelled, brushing flakes off his coat. "Someone is home." Just then, a fierce bark erupted from the pasture behind him. Mannie flashed his phone around the field, illuminating numerous goats and sheep huddled together in a shed. Then his phone lit up a huge white beast with ruffled fur and a long tail.

"A wolf," Mannie yelled as he tore back to the Coffin, slipping and sliding until he reached the car. "Read about wolves, never saw one though," he mumbled breathlessly. He seemed visibly shaken, his teeth chattering, but when he saw the terror in my eyes, he seemed to get a hold of himself and forced a tightlipped smile.

"Wolves eat children, right?" My voice was husky with fear.

"Of course not." Harlo rolled her eyes at Mannie. Maybe it's only a coyote or a guard dog. We are at an animal Shel-ter." She accentuated the word shelter. Boy, she sounded annoyed.

Mannie clicked the chain link gate open. I was horrified to see him set my wicker suitcase and cello case inside the fence on a walkway that appeared to have been recently shoveled, since it only had an inch of snow covering it, and everything else was buried up to two feet.

Harlo walked back to where I waited in the car. "Get out and help, Borgia. Hurry up, it's freezing." Her breath formed little puffs as she flung open the door and half dragged me out, pulling me along through the snow, only letting go of my arm once I was inside the gate and on the walk to the house. My ruby slippers slipped on the slick ice, but somehow I managed to keep my balance. Why were Mannie and Harlo being so mean? Maybe if I did what they wanted, I could get back in the Coffin and get them to drop me off at the houseboat.

"Stick your head through the flip-flop. Tell us what's in there." Harpo's voice sounded syrupy, but I could still detect a sharp, brittle edge. She was nervously winding her scarf tighter and tighter around her neck.

"All right," I agreed numbly, starting to walk slowly toward the stucco building, but I kept an eye on both of them. When I got to the front door, I kicked at the giant flip-flop, sprinkling glitter from my ruby slippers all over the porch. The flip-flop gave easily.

"Unlocked," I yelled.

"Hurrah," Harlo shouted, cupping both hands around her mouth. "Take a peek inside." She sounded more pleasant. Maybe everything would be okay. I bent over and pushed my head through the opening, and was confronted by a speckled tile floor that smelled of cleaner and disinfectant. It looked like a waiting room; several chairs and a long bench lined the walls. Best of all, it was nice and warm. A high counter ran along the back wall and a large cork bulletin board was covered with photos of dogs and cats. In the farthest corner a fake Christmas tree glowed with multicolored lights. Sacks of dog food and boxes of dog treats were piled underneath.

"Keep going," Harlo yelled. "Check the lock on the front door." I did what she said, turned the dead bolt and pulled it open. To my surprise, Mannie and Harlo were clamoring back into the Coffin. Car doors slammed. The motor burst to life, and the tires spun, spewing up snow as the car skidded backwards.

CHAPTER

SIX

"Wait," I screamed. "Don't leave me here." I hurtled down the icy walk, but it was too late. Their car was disappearing. Stunned, I stared at the red tail-lights until they too were swallowed up by the night. From the pasture, the big white beast started barking again.

My teeth chattering, I grabbed my suitcases and dragged them back into the waiting room. Prying open the blinds, I peered out the frosted window and prayed Mannie would come back and get me. The lone streetlight cast a winter glow on a snow lit stage of snowflakes. They no longer reminded me of ballerinas. They looked helpless, cold and undirected.

The frozen chain link fence reminded me of a prison. A heavy dread now pressed on my chest. I could barely move. Was I turning into an icicle? For a few seconds, I gasped for air. "Mom, Mom," I rasped. The heavy ache in my heart was laced with panic that shot through my entire body. My hands started to tremble. I pictured Mom in handcuffs. What had happened to her? Was it because of me?

It was almost like I had fallen off the cliff at the beach-house and tumbled into a snowy nightmare. Worse, I suddenly pictured the hole in our houseboat, bubbling with water. A shiver of terror wracked my body as I imagined myself falling down into that watery hole. The thought of abandonment was so perilous, the homesickness so wretched.

"Mom will call. Mom will call," I rasped over and over. Then I remembered. I had handed Mom's phone to Harlo. Her cell phone was inside Mannie's hearse, resting in the cupholder between the front seats, next to his cracked coffee cup and the butts of Mom's old cigarettes. My eyes blurred; my knees buckled.

I sank down on the linoleum floor next to the fake Christmas tree and leaned against a bag of dog food. The decorations dangled over me, rubbery dog toys and colorful pet ID tags shaped like bones. The room reeked of medicine. A cutout cardboard sign advertising heart worm pills perched on the counter, and the photos of lost dogs pinned to the bulletin board made me feel even worse.

I racked my mind, recalling how I had once made an escape from my babysitter Volly's house. She did not like me. I felt her cold disdain the moment I met her. Her thinning hair was twisted into a knot high on her head, held in place by an outrageously long knitting needle that jabbed dangerously close to my eyes, the few times she leaned over to speak to me, usually only in Mom's presence. Once the adults were gone, Volly ignored me as if I were a piece of furniture that had been placed in her way and needed to be dropped off at the Goodwill.

Whenever I pictured Volly's grotesque face, it was illuminated by a digital screen. Her main activity seemed to be scrolling on her cell phone. She rarely said anything. There were no toys in her house. One afternoon I found a jigsaw puzzle and spent hours trying to work it by myself on the floor. I never got very far, only the corners and some outside edges with a big gap of missing pieces in the middle. A terrible loneliness filled every moment I spent in that dimly lit home. The ache that crept into my heart spread into her faded green curtains and orange carpet. Dread filled me now, as I thought about my lonely time with Volly.

I knew I did not belong with this babysitter, not even for a minute. All her rooms were cluttered with baskets of yarn, with sharp needles poking out. The piles of magazines were all about knitting and sewing. I never saw Volly knit or sew. The worst memory was the pair of salt and pepper shakers set over the kitchen stove, a round man and woman with no arms or legs, each with alarming circular expressions on their red mouths as if they had been poked and cut by scissors. I imagined they were mouthing the word "ouch."

A heavy odor of grease mixed with a scent of fruity soap and some mildewed sponges revolted me. My memory even stirred up the overhead light fixture where trapped houseflies lay feet up or buzzed round and round in the glass. Staring at the dead flies made me think I would never escape, but I had to try.

The next time Mom left me with Volly, I decided to leave a trail like Hansel and Gretel, so I could find my way home. On the way to her house, I sacrificed my favorite-colored candies, dropping them one by one out the back window of the car. Blue, red, green, and yellow pieces dotted the gutter and the curb. After Mom drove away, I waited half an hour, then slipped out the back door and followed the trail of candy home. Crows flew down and grabbed pieces, even a squirrel ran off with one in his mouth, but enough candies were left on the sidewalk to guide me back to the houseboat.

The route I followed was mostly downhill. It took a couple hours to walk all the way back. When people appeared on the sidewalk, I slipped into strangers' front yards and pretended to be playing as if I lived there. I knew to be careful on the steep cement walks and the slippery wooden pier. I was so happy to come upon the shining lake with the white boats bobbing. Mom and Del never locked the houseboat door, so I slipped inside, crawled into my bed and fell fast asleep.

There was a terrible commotion that afternoon, with people alternately screaming at me and hugging me when they discovered me safe under the covers of my red and white quilt. Mom never left me with Volly again. Instead, during shows, I was allowed to hide in the cupboards at the Crocodile Concert Hall. As I got older, Mom even let me stay home alone at the houseboat, with instructions not to open the door for anyone. When asked why I had run away, all I could say was I hated the salt-shakers and knitting needles. Also, it did not smell right. I did not even try to explain the fruity soap and moldy sponges.

"She's definitely your daughter," Del said, looking up from the TV on the momentous day I made my escape from Volly's house. Mom and I were relaxing on the deck, watching Canadian Geese glide by on the water. The houseboat windows and doors were open to catch the breeze. Little birds, blue and orange barn swallows dipped over the surface, occasionally landing on the eaves of the roof. Del leaned out the open window and took a sip of Mom's iced tea. "Volly sounds pretty boring," he said, winking at me, knowing he would set Mom off.

"Shut up," she said, brandishing her finger at Del. "Volly is a perfectly nice lady. Borgia has abandonment issues. I blame her father. For heaven's sakes, she says she was upset by the salt-shakers." Yeah, Mom, I thought, but I escaped. I took charge. I smiled at Del and kept quiet. I was happy to be back with Mom and Del in our wonderful houseboat. I had no memories of my dad, so how could he be to blame?

Now, just like that day I escaped from Volly, I had to form a plan. I curled up like a snail on the floor, trying to think, but was roused by the sound of a car motor. Headlights lit up the back wall, and the bulletin board pet photos were illuminated. My spirit soared.

CHAPTER
SEVEN

"Mannie," I yelled ecstatically. Jumping up, I grabbed my wicker suitcase, threw open the front door and ran haphazardly down the glazed walkway, sinking deeper and deeper in the snow. I didn't care that the air was freezing, that I was not wearing my coat, or that the glaring headlights were blinding me. Holding up my hand, I waved frantically.

Then I realized the headlights were not coming from Mannie's black Coffin, but from a battered red pickup. The motor still running, a man in a puffy jacket and orange stocking cap jumped out and crunched through the snow to the back of the truck. Horrible scraping sounds filled the air as he dragged a crate over the rusted truck bed, until it dropped to the ground. Next, he yanked open the chain link gate and dragged the crate just inside the fence. Inside was a live animal.

"Delivery complete," he said, pulling at his stocking hat while making eye contact with me for the first time. "One giant pup."

I took a few steps back. The so-called pup was frantic, snapping at the wire cage with tortured cries. Blood ran from the dog's mouth. I was horrified by the fear and despair in its eyes.

"New home, Eightball," the man said calmly, glaring at the crate. "Pup's paperwork should be on your computer," he yelled back to me, almost as an afterthought. "Crazy name, Eightball, maybe this dog will tell your fortune." Then he laughed as if he had cracked a funny joke. The laugh evolved into a cough, doubling him over. Still rasping, he managed to slam the tailgate and climb back into the cab. I stood mute, as the truck swerved and fishtailed back down the icy road. Numb with my own abandonment, I ignored the whimpering pup. When the cold finally engulfed me, I trudged back into the warm shelter and locked the door.

I don't know how long I walked round and round that dimly lit room, grasping my wicker suitcase, stepping over the black cello case that lay sprawled out on the floor like a dead body. My sopped ruby slippers left a watery trail of sparkle wherever I stepped. I kept passing a scratched blue door at the back of the reception counter—obviously covered with the paw marks of desperate shelter animals. The blue door seemed the only alternative to staying in this overheated office or going back out in the freezing snowstorm. I took a hold of the doorknob, turned it cautiously, then stepped into a dark hallway.

At the far end of the hall, a washing machine churned round and round. Its sudsy window resembled a watery eye, clouded by tumbling, sopped clothes. The sound of the machine was comforting. I paused to listen, taking a deep breath–when a huge dog sprang out of nowhere. His dark eyes glowed. His lips curled back, revealing sharp fangs. A menacing growl wracked the creature's entire body. His wedge-shaped face with dark brindled stripes made him look more like a tiger than a dog. Suddenly the beast lunged, snapping only inches from my face. Instinctively, I held up my wicker suitcase like a shield and stumbled backwards, screaming, as the dog clamped the edge of the suitcase in its jaws and snapped off a protruding Barbie arm.

In that second, another dog stepped from the shadows, a mottled black and grey dog with a narrow snout and strange light eyes. Instead of lunging, the new dog turned and faced the wedge-faced creature head on. It positioned itself between me and the snarling beast. Deep growls filled the room. The hair on the smaller dog stood straight up. Baring its teeth, it froze into position, every muscle tensed. The wedge-faced creature began to waver. One last hollow growl rattled from its throat. Then he snapped his mouth closed and bolted down the dark corridor, past wire cages that set off a cacophony of howls and yips. At the last moment, the brindle dog tucked his tail between his legs and crashed through a giant flip flop in the door at the end of the hall.

My heart pounded in my ears. I tried to catch my breath. The grey and black dog now turned and faced me, its light eyes glowing. I swallowed. Terrified, I froze as the dog crouched down to the ground and crawled forward on its belly, pulling back its lips, revealing its white teeth in a grotesque smile. When the animal reached me, it stood up and grabbed my wrist in its mouth. I screamed, expecting sharp pain, but there were no sharp teeth in the grasp. This was not a bite. Instead, the dog pulled me awkwardly forward, and I tripped and stumbled after it.

In the far corner of the shadowy room, directly in front of the sloshing machine, a matted pillow was crowded with grey and black puppies, miniature versions of the mottled dog. The fat puppies slept in various states, some on the pillow, some on the floor, a few upside-down, one with four legs in the air. The pups slept soundly, immune to the commotion, although occasionally a stubby leg flailed the air as if a puppy dream were fretful. Soft yelps occasionally sounded, but not a pup awakened.

The mottled dog, obviously the mother, collapsed down on the bare floor and glanced up at me sympathetically. I stared at the pillow full of sleeping puppies, and then I collapsed down at the pillow's edge, careful not to crush a fat tummy or a tiny head. Above me, the soggy clothes churned round and round, while I perched in a stiff and troubled trance, the mother dog near me, alert and on guard.

I came out of my stupor when the puppies awoke and began to squirm all over me. Their sweet puppy breath smelled like perfume. I touched all the pink stomachs, cradled each one. I tried to think what to do next, but it was as if a terrible black curtain had turned off all the lights in my mind, blacked out my ability to focus on anything but what was right in front of me. Thankfully at this moment, I was surrounded by puppies.

The puppies continued to swarm over me, licking my face and hands, even trying out their sharp little needle teeth, tugging on my already tattered Esmeralda costume. Infused by their warmth, some of the frozen ice inside me began to thaw. Puppies are pure happiness. Their mother, who had remained at a distance with her head on her paws, suddenly advanced and lay down in the middle of the giant pillow. All the little creatures tumbled and bumbled to her side to nurse. They pushed and scrabbled at each other, closing their eyes with pleasure as their mother's milk entered their tiny pink mouths. I stood up and turned awkwardly around, staring at my feet. The washing machine had stopped turning. The wet clothes lay piled in the window.

I tried to take stock of my predicament. I was at an animal shelter. Mom was gone. Del was gone. The police were involved. I was alone. The puppies were content with their mother, but I was not a puppy, and I was not with my mother. My mom's words came back to me. "Borgia has abandonment issues. Don't worry kiddo. I will never leave you." Mom's broken promise haunted me. She had left me, just like my dad I could hardly remember. To top it off, I was abandoned in the strangest place I had ever been.

I towered over the puppies like a clumsy giant. As they nursed, I grabbed my wicker suitcase and set it on top of the washing machine. Then I peered down the hall lined by a corridor of metal kennels. At the far end of the hall, a narrow bar of light radiated under the door, illuminating the giant flip-flop where the brindled dog had disappeared. Hesitantly, I walked past the gauntlet of barking dogs in their cages, and lifted the flip flop, poking my head through to look around.

CHAPTER
EIGHT

The room lay in murky shadow. A huge Christmas tree glowed in the corner, its multicolored lights reflected in the floor-to-ceiling windows. Unlike the fake tree in the front office decorated with dog treats, this huge fir tree was real, and covered with all manner of glistening red and silver ornaments. At the tiptop of the tree, a large angel, missing its head, was wrapped in a mass of feathery white. I gasped as the angel started to move. A head appeared, and two beady eyes glared down at me. My mistake—this was no angel, but a living parrot. The bird flapped its wings and leaned over to get a better look. Its awkward movement caused the top branches to shift, and several ornaments crashed to the floor.

Mesmerized, I crawled into the room and stood up. Christmas music played softly, punctuated by loud snorts and snores. As my eyes grew accustomed to the dim light, I realized the sofa was packed, not with decorative pillows as I first thought, but sleeping dogs of all shapes and sizes, many of them wearing colorful jackets that made them look more like decorations. Alarmed, I knew I should leave, but I could not bring myself to turn away.

ZZZZ, Snort, Plop—crazy sounds rose from every corner of the room. In the center, a single pole lamp beamed down on a ripped and torn leather recliner, where a solitary human figure dozed, her furry slippers cast high in the air. A drooping head obscured her face. I shifted my gaze to a card table covered with puzzle pieces and gasped. Was this sleeping woman my dreaded babysitter Volly? The half-worked puzzle brought back memories of many homesick hours. What if Volly had moved to the suburbs? What if Mom had arranged for Mannie to leave me with her again? I had to get a better look.

I tiptoed forward, past the piles of slumbering dogs. To my amazement, the animals continued to sleep peacefully. I was grateful to have recently studied dogs in homeschool. Now I used my studies to identify the various breeds. An upside-down pug snored loudly on a pillow. What seemed to be a wiry Schnauzer lay under an end table, its four legs splayed, its head resting on a rubber bone. A grand, short haired dog with jowls dozed, its body draped half on and off the sofa, maybe a mastiff? Across the top of the sofa, an array of fluff ball dogs curled together in shades ranging from white to apricot--their faces hidden by their curly coats. Pressed against the back sliding door, I recognized the wedge-faced dog that had confronted me earlier. It was now sleeping like a baby.

Behind the lounger, a great black dog lay flat on its stomach. It resembled a giant bear rug, spread out on top of the green carpet. Curled up with this great dog was a much smaller creature, half buried in the larger dog's dense coat. A Labrador retriever with a grey muzzle stretched out asleep near the fireplace. I had never seen so many dogs.

A warning alarm pulsed in my brain, telling me to retreat, get out of the room while I could. Instead, I took a few steps closer. I wanted to make sure the solitary human figure was not my dreaded babysitter from the past. As I neared the edge of the card table, relief flooded me from head to toe. This was definitely not Volly, but some other strange woman, wearing giant headphones and a velvet bathrobe embroidered with green leaves and red cherries. Her rust-colored hair frizzed out in all directions, and huge round spectacles magnified her closed eyes, so that she looked like a dozing owl.

It was a miracle I did not wake the dogs or this woman. I gazed down at the half-worked puzzle on the card table, revealing the face of a young girl. Her straw-colored hair stuck straight out behind her as if the wind was pulling it away from her. I reached down to pick up a puzzle piece that had fallen on the floor, when a diabolical laugh pierced my ears. A rasping voice cackled "bad girl, dirty girl" followed by wicked laughter. I closed my hand around the puzzle piece and crouched below the card table's spindly legs, trying to hide.

Was the woman in the flowered robe speaking to me? Did she think I was breaking into her house? Were the dogs going to awake and attack? The cackling voice sounded like a witch. Then I realized the haranguing voice came from the top of the Christmas tree and belonged to the white parrot. Suddenly the bird dove straight at me, spreading the yellow underside of his white wings as he dipped across the room, cackling hysterically.

During that tumultuous flight, the parrot voice changed to the most yowling deranged cat cries I had ever heard. "Meowwwww, meowww." Like a shot, all the dogs awoke and sprang to attention. "Cat! Cat!" their dog brains seemed to say. Hysterical barks, woofs, snarls, yelps filled the room, and dogs of every size gyrated and jumped, trying to snap at the crazed parrot where he now perched on the padded top of the recliner.

CHAPTER
NINE

I jumped up, nearly knocking over the card table. Scrambling across the room, I dove through the flip-flop, clamored down the hall, and madly pulled myself up on top of the washing machine. My knees folded against my chest, I grabbed a blue spray bottle of bleach in one hand and a yellow bottle of stain remover in the other. I aimed both bottles like drawn pistols, prepared to defend myself. The pup's mother cocked her head curiously, while her puppies slept peacefully through all the barking and alarms.

"Silence," a female voice commanded. "Enough!" I peeked around the corner to see the red-haired woman from the recliner standing in her bathrobe, only a few feet away. She flipped the switch on the wall, and light flooded the room. The terrible white parrot perched on her shoulder, leaned forward, its beady eyes glowing, the yellow feathers on its head, rising dramatically.

A few final woofs sounded. Dogs leapt in the air, turning in circles and a black and white terrier tugged on the woman's slippers. With one fell swoop, she swept all the animals into the room behind her, slammed the door in their faces, then reached down and latched the flip-flop.

I pulled my head back, closed my eyes and pushed my body against the hard dials of the washing machine, praying the woman had not seen me. The mother dog wagged her tail. When I opened my eyes, the frizzle haired woman stood directly in front of me. The white parrot craned his head and clicked his beak. Lifting a sharp talon, he pointed at me, and began to repeat the same chant over and over, "Bad girl, dirty girl." Then he performed a little two-step dance, the crest on his head moving up and down as he made a mechanical sound of the sopping clothes churning round and round in the washing machine. The strange woman leaned closer, peering at me as if she could not believe her eyes. I gripped my bottles tight, ready to spray.

"Hush, Typhoon," the woman said, placing her hand over the parrot's beak. She removed her owl-like glasses as if that might change what she saw. Then her mouth fell open in surprise, "Good Heavens, dear child, what are you doing on top of my washing machine?"

For a moment every muscle in my body tensed, my eyes widened, my jaw set. My fingers on the triggers, I aimed the spray bottles right at her face, but some sweet quality in her voice melted my resolve. I dropped the bottles. One fell to the floor. "I don't know," I managed to sputter. "I was dropped off here."

The woman blinked. She pushed her glasses back up on her nose, her green eyes now intensely magnified by the thick lenses. Then she placed one hand dramatically over her heart as if my words had pierced it, and with the other hand, set the white parrot on a perch next to the dryer. There the bird continued to raise and lower his yellow head feathers as he paced back and forth, clicking his beak and fluffing himself up to twice his normal size.

In one sweeping move, the strange woman reached out and wrapped her arms around me. She smelled of chocolate and dog biscuits, of cherry cough drops and puppies. Her thick flowered robe was as soft as a cloud. I buried my face in the embroidered green leaves and red cherries. Her tender embrace was too much. I began to cry.

"There, there," the lady said. "Everything will be all right. You are my Christmas gift tonight, dear child. I am Maya." She stepped back and shook my hand as if we were being introduced at a party.

"Borgia," I said, allowing her to take my limp hand. "Borgia OftheGlades."

"Magnificent name," the lady said, clapping her hand over her mouth. "Come down from the washer, right now. Let me help you." I slid to the edge of the washing machine, pulling some lint and sheets of fabric softener off my clothes, realizing my Esmeralda costume had been torn and shredded by the puppies crawling and pulling at me. The woman gently lifted me down, took my hand and led me back through the door to the room of thrashing, exuberant dogs. None of them barked now. There were dogs in plaid coats and Santa jackets, sparkling jeweled collars, felt antlers and elf hats. Some even wore blue and white outfits, I decided must be for Hanukkah.

"Where is your home?" Maya asked as she led me past all the animals. "Did you already tell me, and I forgot? I can be quite forgetful, dear."

"At the Space Needle," I said, realizing that was not a clear answer. I should have said near the Space Needle, but my mind was not working. I could feel my lower lip begin to quiver.

Maya's left eyebrow shot up. It dawned on me that most

people would yell, "Liar," or tell me to quit imagining, but Maya just seemed intrigued.

"High up in the air?" she asked.

"No, under the Space Needle." That part was true. Our lake shore houseboat had a fabulous view of the famous Seattle tower built for a long-ago World's Fair.

"How did you manage to get clear out here to this dog shelter on such a snowy night?" Maya looked amazed.

"Mannie's Coffin." When I saw Maya's brow furrow again, I added. "The Coffin is actually an old hearse, you know, a car used to carry dead bodies to funerals. Now it carries musical instruments and musician to concerts."

"What?" Maya had such a quizzical look on her face.

"Mannie and Harlo were driving. Mom's friends. They dropped me off here."

"Oh!" Maya looked around the room. "Well, you are not alone. Every dog you see was dropped off. You must have already met Metzy, our mother dog, and her puppies."

I nodded and folded my arms protectively against my chest.

"Metzy was left, just before she delivered her pups." While Maya talked, I looked down to see all the dogs were vying for my attention. It was as if they thought I was one of them. They greeted me with pink tongues and thumping tails.

"Careful, careful," Maya said, pushing away a dog here and there, but she did not stop the shower of affection. Then she pulled a cell phone out of her pocket. "Would you like me to call someone, dear? I could call the police and let them...."

"No," I screamed, and dissolved into a puddle on the floor, imploring her with folded hands. "Please, please don't call the police." Maya looked perplexed. She slipped her cellphone back in her pocket.

"Don't be alarmed," she said. "I want to help you. You can stay here as long as you like. The road just closed moments ago anyway. No one else will make it up our hill tonight. Too dangerous. I won't call the police."

I let out a big sigh and stood up. "I like the police," I said. "A friendly policeman used to give me popsicles, but my mom told me not to call them tonight."

Just then, a great black dog sat up behind the recliner. The hair on top of his head stood straight up on end. He looked worried. "That's Nemo, the Newfoundland, our largest dog at 150 pounds. Be careful, dear. He drools long, slimy ropes. He might accidentally knock you over, but Nemo will never hurt you on purpose. He is our most gentle soul."

"He was dropped off?" This big dog seemed so grand, so gorgeous.

"All the dogs were."

"Why?"

"No good reason," Maya's forehead furrowed. She set her earphones on the card table. "When Nemo gets excited, he accidentally bumps people. He likes to sit in the driver's seat of cars. When he falls asleep, his giant head leans on the horn, making a racket. Nemo also likes to drink out of the toilet, then slobbers all over the house. He climbed on his owner's white sofa, leaving stains. Newfoundlands are a bit oily. On a positive note, they happen to be excellent swimmers and love to rescue drowning people."

Maya walked behind the sofa and petted Nemo on his grand bear-like head. His eyes were bloodshot. He looked pathetic and sad. "Such a loyal dog, he still misses his former owner," she whispered. "Most dogs form strong bonds with their humans."

"Terrible," I said, staring at Nemo, but feeling sorry mostly for myself.

"Yes," Maya went on, "There was no good reason to leave him behind, but his owner thought the big dog was too difficult and gave him up. None of us are perfect. Thank heavens.

A few faults here, a few faults there, make the world go around."

She began to try and cool herself with a paper fan decorated with green bamboo shoots. "My, it's warm in here. Perhaps being left behind is the way to mix the world up a little. Leaves fall off trees. Balloons float away. Maybe being left behind isn't so bad." I did not agree with this idea at all, but somehow the images were comforting. Listening to Maya, I felt better.

Just then there was a loud meow that seemed to come from the ceiling. The parrot again? But when I looked up, I saw a grey cat with green eyes, four black feet and a fluffy tail that stuck straight up like a flag. The haughty cat walked along a narrow ledge, high up in the air, his nose tilted up as if he thought those beneath him were not worthy. He walked along the ledge with perfect ease and balance.

"Greet," Maya said waving her hand. "He likes to show off up there on his catwalk. Greet wants you to admire him."

"Why is he up way up there?" I asked.

"One cat living with all these dogs needs to have his own space," Maya said. "Greet prefers to stay up high near the ceiling, while the dogs are down low on the ground. Greet so enjoys antagonizing dogs, antagonizing me, too." The puffball cat paused mid-step as if to prove Maya's point. With one foot elevated, he froze as if he were a stuffed animal rather than a real cat. Then he sank down gracefully, stuck a leg straight out and licked his fur with a dainty pink tongue. Two small dogs barked at him, and he shot them a withering glance.

"Is Greet the only cat?" I asked.

"Yes, like I am the only woman, and you are the only girl." Maya smiled at her own words, and the warmth of that smile melted even more of the frost in my soul. I could feel the muscles in my neck relax. For a moment, just a moment, my mouth curved toward a smile, maybe more like the sliver of a faraway moon. My body was still heavy and numb. I felt anxious, but the hint, even just a sprinkle of something positive, made me feel better. Maya seemed to notice the change and looked relieved.

"Dear girl," she said, "see this puzzle I'm working?" I nodded and gazed down at all the red and black pieces spread out on the card table. I focused on the girl whose hair seemed to be blowing. Maya picked up the lid of the puzzle box and studied it. "Here is a picture of the completed puzzle. It's a copy of an old painting. Guess what happened to this girl?"

I shrugged. "I don't know."

"Left behind," Maya peered at me through her owl glasses. "In fact, the artist titled the painting, *The Girl I left Behind Me.* Her face grew soft and kind. "I love mystery," she said. "Life is mysterious." Her eyes got larger and rounder, as she traced her finger over the rough pieces that fit together, forming a strange, old-fashioned child standing on the edge of a cliff. "See how all alone the girl is?"

"She looks cold." I said, still feeling cold myself.

"Yes, a wicked wind blowing in the painting. Her hair is totally out of control. Hmm, we seem to be missing a piece right here, where her hands should be."

"Oh." I dug in my pocket and produced the piece I had picked up off the floor. I handed it to Maya.

"Good job! You saved it from the dogs. Let's see if it fits." Pointing with her finger, Maya handed the piece back to me. "It looks like books."

I slipped the piece into the empty space. It fit perfectly. Maya held up a magnifying glass, so she could see the girl holding the books close to her heart. "Excellent work, Borgia," she said, setting the glass down on the table.

I looked around. I didn't know what to say. I stared at the

torn and scratched lounger. It obviously had been chewed on by dogs.

"My chair has a remote control," Maya said, watching me. 'Try it." She handed me a device, so I eased down on the cracked cushions and pushed buttons that made it tip back and lift up my feet. A circle of dogs watched intently, while Maya continued to work on the puzzle.

"The artist never sold the painting. The girl's identity is an unsolved mystery, because the painter died without telling anyone her name." Maya seemed to be talking more to herself than to me.

"A real girl?" I asked, pushing buttons to bring the chair into an upright position.

"Yes," Maya turned the puzzle box over and ran her finger along the back. "The artist was Eastman Johnson. I'm sure he felt bad about leaving this lovely girl behind. When you leave someone behind, you suffer. Someone is missing you right now, I am sure."

"My mom," I said, my eyes welling with tears.

"Of course," Maya said. "You mother misses you very much. We have to find the pieces to your puzzle and fit you back together."

I sniffled a bit and tried to sink down in the lounge chair, embarrassed to be crying in front of a stranger.

Maya handed me some tissues and kept talking, "This girl is a symbol for all people left behind. Everyone suffers, Borgia. Time leaves us all behind one way or another, but we take a few steps forward and keep going." Maya blinked and her green eyes stared into space as if the advice was for herself, not me. "Will you help me finish working this puzzle?" She looked down at me. I nodded.

Just then a fat pug in a plaid jacket leapt onto the card table, snatched a puzzle piece in his mouth and tore over the card table, breaking up some of the worked section. The little dog challenged us, his eyes dancing as if he wanted us to laugh at his destruction. Then he plopped right down on top of the table, panting, a piece hidden in the folds of his mouth.

"Drop it. Drop it," Maya commanded. She grabbed the dog by his ham-shaped body, held him upside down and shook. A puzzle piece, wet and swollen, dropped from his mouth, but as it fell, a droopy eared bassett hound poked its head from under the table, cracked open its mouth and swallowed it whole. Then the bassett looked up at Maya and wagged its tail as if it expected praise.

"Now the puzzle will never be complete," Maya said, talking again more to herself than to me, "but it's all right." She held up both hands, shook her head and exhaled. "Dogs are not perfect. It's Christmas, let it be."

She fell back into her recliner, rubbing her forehead and humming a Beatle song that even I recognized. Feeling a little awkward, I walked over and sat down on the edge of the blanket-covered sofa. Immediately, a pug jumped into my lap and licked my face. White hair flew out in all directions. I tried to wrestle the dog away, but it curled up on my lap like a loaded spring and stuck out a pink tongue, panting happily.

"I'm sorry for such bad manners," Maya said. "Pugs tend to lose their hair when excited." She fanned the air, trying to clear away the tufts of dog hair drifting all around us. A black and white terrier now tugged on my sock. The huge mastiff with sagging jowls leaned sadly against my leg and drooled.

"Oh, Mobley," Maya said, nodding towards the huge dog. "He gets so morose when a small dog like Crumpet can fit into people's laps and he can't. Mastiffs are just too big. It's all right, darling."

When Mobley heard his name, he walked stiffly over to Maya as if his back legs hurt. She rubbed his grey head, furrowed with wrinkles, and wiped away his drool with a paper towel.

"That's Georgia, next to you and Crumpet in your lap," Maya said smiling. "Crumpet was left behind when she kept jumping on the table. She often ate her owner's prescription pills causing all kinds of drama. The darling is a bit overweight. She also loves butter and can swallow an entire cube whole. Pugs love to run away from home, unlike Nemo the Newfoundland over there, who hates to leave his living space."

Maya tried to convince me I could make friends with the wedge-faced dog, Slider. I gave him a pat. He didn't growl, but I didn't trust him. I also met Gizmo, the Schnauzer and the black chow mix, Gobi, with a blue tongue. "Gobi imagines himself a Newfoundland," Maya confided. "He prefers to hang out with the big dogs."

Two small fluff dogs, Rolly and Jazz, wore red and pink jackets with jeweled collars. Their eyes were hard to see under their fluffy fur, but they wagged their tails and licked my hand. The black Labrador mix, Jounce, was an older, calm soul who wagged his whole body but did not jump on me, unlike the smaller dogs who kept plopping into my lap.

The Bassett hound, Deville, of the droopy eyes and long ears, lay in one place under the card table, seemingly too tired or too lazy to move, but I noted how quickly her mouth had opened when she had an opportunity to swallow a puzzle piece.

I could hardly keep the dogs straight as Maya led me past the kennels in the hall.

"These new drop offs need to be socialized before they join the family," she said. "Dogs come and go here. We try to find them forever homes."

" Only some dogs wear jackets," I remarked.

"Right. The small shorthaired dogs are often too cold. The big thick haired dogs are often too warm. Pugs and poodles go both ways. I get hot and cold too. I try to find a middle tempera-ture." She laughed and fanned herself. "Before the dogs go to bed, some of them are going to put on a holiday show. Are you ready to join the audience?"

"I guess," I said stiffly. I sat up, dried my eyes and blew my nose.

"Choir," Maya yelled, holding up a sparkly children's wand and a bulging paper bag. Instantly, about a third of the dogs snapped to attention. Mouths closed, eyes focused, ears pricked forward. Order lasted about three seconds, while all the other dogs watched.

Then a long, low dachshund mix snapped at a pug. The pug snapped at a Jack Russell, and three little dogs snapped at the giant Newfoundland Nemo who sat quietly and snapped at no one. When a small dog tried to bite him, he simply raised his thick neck higher, keeping his eyes glued to the treat bag.

"Perform," Maya commanded, alternately waving her wand and shaking the bag of treats. Three fluff ball dogs, in shades of white, orange and cream, jumped on the sofa and sat up. "Pugs," she shouted and two fawn-colored dogs with curled tails performed handstands. Maya's wand moved to the black and white Jack Russell terriers who gyrated in the air, flipping their muscular little bodies in an amazing display of gymnas-tics. "Mastiff," Maya cried, and the giant Mobley made a half-hearted attempt to roll over, but he paused on his back, his legs in midair, looking like he had just expired. All the other dogs sat or lay watching the performance. "Their role is to be a good audience," Maya said.

Just then, one of the pugs darted out of the bathroom with a toilet paper roll unfurling as he ran through the house. "Not planned," Maya said in exasperation as the Basset snapped at the winding paper banner, tearing it to shreds. Bits of tissue flew in all directions. "Discipline," Maya shouted. She fished a silver whistle out of her pocket and blew. Then she glanced at me. I clapped. I wished I could smile, but I couldn't. Mom would say, "Get over yourself, Borgia."

"Choir," she yelled and blew two tweets.

A few small dogs jumped onto the rim of the sofa. Two medium dogs piled on the sofa cushions, and two huge dogs lay down on the floor, Nemo at one end and Mobley at the other. All the other dogs looked on from their perches.

Maya eased down on a piano bench and lifted her hands dramatically. "Sing," she commanded as she pounded out a jangly version of "Jingle Bells." Some of the dogs began to howl. It was terrible. Maya glanced back at me and raised her eyebrows dramatically.

I clapped again. The dogs were so awful, I almost smiled.

Maya pulled out a handkerchief. "Too hot, too hot," she said, wiping away beads of perspiration from her forehead. "Break! Time for a tour of the house with no dogs allowed." She pulled the living room door closed behind her and pointed out a bedroom down a short hall. Then she led me into a kitchen and up a steep flight of wooden stairs to a small room piled high with stacks of books, puzzles and DVDs.

"There's a bed under here somewhere," Maya muttered, moving magazines and boxes. "You can sleep in this guest room. How does that sound?"

I didn't know what to say. Maya left me alone in the cluttered room, but she soon returned with clean, sweet smelling sheets and a blue vase brimming with green holly dotted with red berries. She set the arrangement on the dresser next to a black Eightball–the kind you shake to get watery answers to any questions you ask.

"Eightball," I said, suddenly remembering the pup left out in the snow.

CHAPTER
TEN

"Maya," I exclaimed. "A dog was dropped off here tonight, a big black pup."

"What?" Maya frowned. "Where?" She stopped fluffing the bed pillows and faced me, both hands on her hips.

"Outside by the front gate." I felt terrible. I had left the poor dog in the snow.

"Great Gravy," Maya exclaimed, "so fortuitous."

"Fortu—what?" I said.

"Nothing, dear. Let's go. What a Christmas Eve this is turning out to be."

She threw a puffy jacket around my shoulders and exchanged her long green robe for a full-length parka with a hood. Then she pulled on a pair of gum boots and thick gloves, grabbing a flashlight from the dresser.

We found the dog crate under the solitary streetlight, with the great black pup hunkered down and shivering. As soon as he saw us, he began to whimper and whine. He threw himself against the cage, biting the wires, so that blood flowed from his muzzle, staining the snow red.

"This will never do," Maya said. She pried open the latch, immediately freeing the dog, who bounded out wagging his tail. He tore through the snow, returning to bounce off us energetically, as if to say, thank you, thank you for setting me free. Finally, he settled down next to me and pawed at my leg.

"He likes you, Borgia." Maya studied the black dog carefully.

I stared at the giant pup, about to explain about the delivery man, but the words that came out of my mouth surprised me, "Can I help take care of him?"

"Of course," Maya said. "He can sleep in your room to night—get to know you."

My eyes widened. "The pup can sleep with me?"

"No more cages for him. You can see he is severely traumatized by being in that crate. Not all dogs can handle being caged. Call him, Borgia."

I bit my lip. How did you call a dog? The pup was bounding up and down in the snow. "Eightball," I yelled. That was what the man in the truck had called him. To my amazement, he came thudding to my side and plopped down, thumping a snow-covered tail. Then he raised a cold paw, hitting me in the knee.

"Yes, indeed," Maya said. "Anyone can see this fella likes you. He may be your Christmas present. My mother was Norwegian, so we always opened our presents on Christmas Eve, a perfect time for you to get a present, but it's late. I'm weary. We can talk about this in the morning."

A present for me on Christmas Eve! As I settled under the clean sheets and warm blankets, I had one hand on the head of a giant pup curled up next to me in the bed, taking up half the space. Before I knew it, I was asleep. In the middle of the night, I awoke to a dreadful sound. Eightball sat by the door, his head tipped back, howling miserably. I crawled out of bed, and the pup lowered himself sorrowfully to the ground, as if he expected to be punished.

"Eightball," I said, and hugged his sturdy black body while he licked my face. I sat with him for a long time, my arm around his neck and his broad back. Finally, he curled up and fell back asleep. I crawled back to bed, and for the first time since I had been left behind, I did not think about my own loneliness. Instead, I considered the sad pup and how he needed someone to comfort him. I wondered who he was missing—certainly not the delivery guy in the truck.

CHAPTER
ELEVEN

When I awoke the next morning, I was disoriented. I did not recognize the wallpaper covered with blue and orange dragonflies. A funny, old-fashioned dresser with a mirror stood opposite my bed, almost hidden by piles of books and boxes of jigsaw puzzles. Potted houseplants sat on top of the stacks, with only a narrow trail to the closed door. For a few seconds, my mind spun as if it did not know how to focus. Then I remembered. I had been dropped off at a dog shelter.

All the memories of the previous night came flooding back—me dancing on stage in the velvet curtains, Mom being led away by the police, the Coffin with Mannie driving while snowflakes twirled, the washing machine slogging, a parrot heckling and all the crazy dogs. Somehow, I had been saved by a mother dog with light eyes and a woman named Maya who wore thick glasses that made her look like an owl.

"Mom," I cried out. "Mom, Mom." Then I recalled that the giant pup Eightball, who had slept with me, was missing. I crawled from my crumpled bed and timidly made my way through the stacks and piles, then edged down the steep wooden steps.

"Merry Christmas, Borgia," Maya smiled, as she stepped in from the back hall, wearing gum boots and thick rubber gloves. Her wild red hair was pulled back with a clip. Behind her a grey garden hose snaked down the hallway. She motioned me to follow, her and I watched as she sprayed the kennel floors with stiff blasts of water.

"Worried about Eightball?" She glanced up at me. "He woke up early. Pups need to pee every few hours. Nemo made friends with him right away. The pup is so large, I think he must be part Newfoundland." I listened, but my mind was far away. I was thinking about Mom.

"The kennel dogs are loose in the pasture, romping in the snow. Once I finish cleaning out these kennels, we will have a little time to ourselves."

I stared at my bare feet. "I need to go home," I said hollowly. "I want to call my mother."

"Yes, yes," Maya said. "We can work on that. We need to figure out all the details. This morning I will contact the local police and...."

"Not the police," I cried. "Please, you can't call the police." I pictured Mom in handcuffs and the policeman's haunting words, "You have the right to remain silent." What did that mean? I was at the animal shelter because of Mom's instructions. Maybe a call to the police would be all right, but just the mention of them, gave me a feeling of dread. I felt panicky, just like frantic Eightball trapped in his metal crate. I was desperate to see my mother, but I did not want to get her in trouble. I should not have been on stage at the music concert. The police could see me, twirling in the curtains. I must be to blame.

"The police arrested my mom after her music concert," I

said abruptly. "If you call them, she may get in more trouble. I hope she will call here. Can we wait a little longer?"

Maya studied my face. "We can wait. The road is still closed, and it is Christmas. You think your mom knows to call this shelter?" She looked puzzled.

"I think so. I am not sure."

"Let's have breakfast. Then we can talk about it."

"All right." I felt odd. It did not seem like Christmas.

"I'm making waffles," Maya said. "Do you like waffles?"

Normally I loved waffles, but nothing sounded good. I followed Maya into the kitchen. A big stone sat in my stomach.

"I keep forgetting I can ask you questions," Maya said. "Dogs don't talk. They can't answer me, at least not very well. Luckily, you can. After breakfast, you can join me on my morning walk, and we can discuss the best way to get you back to your mom."

I listened to Maya but did not reply. I managed to eat one waffle topped with butter, syrup and a few fresh strawberries. Then Maya asked me to choose a dog to take on the walk.

"Eightball," I said without thinking.

"Usually I don't take pups, but Eightball is a special case. We will make an exception. In the end, Maya chose the two pugs, Crumpet and Georgia, Jounce the Lab mix, Deville, the bassett and Nemo the Newfoundland. The chosen dogs could hardly bear the joy of being chosen to go on a walk. They jumped and turned. They chased their tails. Maya handed me two leashes. I was in charge of Eightball and Nemo. "Eightball has obviously been on leash before," Maya said, watching him cavort. "See how excited he is, just like the older dogs."

As we set out with the dogs pulling on their leashes, we walked along the boundary of the property. Behind us, a chorus of incredible lonely howls emanated from the shelter. The aggressive Jack Russells snarled and snapped, barking at us as if we were the enemy.

"Why are they so upset?" I asked, as I tried to keep my leashes from tangling while the dogs pulled and twisted in all directions. Even the basset hound, Deville, came alive, tail up, ears flapping.

"Dogs left behind feel bad," Maya said. I knew exactly how they felt.

Maya paused and all the dogs looked up at her as she stared off in the distance. "Ahead is a walking trail with no cars to get in our way."

We walked along the tire tracks in the road and soon stepped into the forest, walking down a snowy trail framed by towering Douglas fir trees. Each branch was weighed down in white, leaning down to earth as if bowing to us. As we approached the entrance to the popular walking trail, the dogs lunged forward, all trying to be first, pulling and peeing on every object in sight. They sniffed each bush and fallen branch and tried to eat pinecones, exposed blades of grass, plastic and paper trash.

I slipped twice on the ice but managed to hold on to the leashes and be pulled along. After walking under a shady canopy of fir branches, the wide trail opened up to pastures and fields. In the distance I could see a spectacular view of white mountain peaks. Occasionally, we passed other people out walking, some with dogs like us.

"Cascade Mountains to the east," Maya said, "Olympics to the west."

"All covered in snow like Mount Rainier," I added.

"Yes, and of course volcanos all around," Maya smiled. "Hopefully, none of these mountains blow their tops today." As we walked, I could see my breath in little puffs. We passed acres and acres of fenced pasture where horses and goats were pawing at the snow, trying to get down to some grass. Hay bales had been dumped in some of the fields, and the goats had dry strands protruding from their mouths.

"Blackberry bushes," I said, noting the snow-covered thickets that bordered the fences. I love blackberries."

"Look, another surprise." Maya pointed her mitten.

I squinted. Off in the distance between two fir trees, I saw a beloved shape. "The Space Needle," I cried in astonishment. I also recognized the tall high-rise buildings of Seattle on the horizon, and could barely make out the three towers on Queen Anne Hill. Seattle! Hope fluttered in my soul. I momentarily felt lighter on my feet. Somehow, I could go home again The city was close enough to be in sight. I was not so lost after all.

Maya smiled broadly. "Seattle is our neighbor."

I nodded, my mind racing. If I followed this trail, I could get back home to the city. As if Maya could read my mind, she said, "Remember, dear, there is a great lake down there between you and your houseboat. We are on the east side of that lake. You will have to cross one of the floating bridges to get home."

"Or take a boat."

"A boat?" Maya said skeptically.

"Yes, I was on one of the Christmas ships two nights ago."

"You were? One of the holiday boats?"

"A big white yacht." I stood still, captivated by the outline of the saucer-like Space Needle, even though it looked about three inches tall and only a ghostly shadow of itself. The hopeful sight made me feel like talking. "My mom is in a rock band," I blurted out. "She and her boyfriend Del played Christmas music for the people on the yacht."

Maya looked surprised. "What is your mother's name?"

"Celia."

Maya's face blanched. She dropped several of the leashes

and placed a red mitten to her cheek. "What is your last name again? I know you told me last night?"

"OftheGlades," I said, rubbing my hand where the leash had raised a blister. Maya frowned, so I repeated more slowly, "Of-the-Glades." I enunciated each syllable.

"Is that your mother's last name?"

"No, her last name is Harringa."

Maya looked relieved. "Harringa," she said. "I don't know any Harringas. Is that her married name?"

"Nope, Mom picked the name out of an online phone book. She liked the sound of Harringa."

That information seemed to disturb Maya. She closed her eyes and stood very still, as if what I said, had just given her a headache. Meanwhile, the dogs ran in all directions, dragging their leashes through the snow, barking and scampering up and down the trail.

"Do you know my mother?"

"I might." Then Maya shook her head and leaned down to pick up her mittens. "No, No, I don't think so. Celia Harringa, I'm sure I do not."

When Maya dropped the leashes, the pugs took off like a shot, running straight toward the goats, barking hysterically as if they had to protect us from a vile enemy. By contrast, Nemo the giant Newfoundland sat down and waited. The hair on his head stood straight up and twirled in the brisk morning breeze. He looked troubled by the other dogs' wild antics. His blood-shot eyes and thick jowls drooped.

The Lab-mix Jounce ran pell-mell toward a half-frozen pond and plunged in, breaking through thin ice, splashing and crashing in the icy muck. Eightball strayed a few feet away and began to gobble up fresh horse manure as if he was starving. I tried to pull him away.

"Stop, stop," I yelled. Ears flapping, the basset hound Deville bayed as she ran down the trail, chasing a rabbit.

"Oh dear," Maya handed me some dry dog kibbles from her coat pocket. "Yell 'Treat' and the pugs will come running." One of her mittens had fallen to the ground again.

I handed Eightball's leash to Maya and ran after the enraged pugs, yelling "treat, treat." Immediately, the little dogs spun around. Their ears perked up, their tails curled. Snorting and huffing, they ran toward me on stubby legs. As they passed the patient Nemo, they lunged at his neck, and snapped wildly. Nemo ignored the snarling pugs, lifted his furry neck and continued to stare at Maya. Eightball tucked his tail between his legs fearfully when they snarled, but he was already twice the size of the pugs and had little to worry about from their tantrums.

Finally all the dogs were collected. We brushed the snow off a giant boulder and sat down to rest. I continued to stare at the outline of the skyscrapers and the Space Needle shimmering in a mist on the horizon.

"Would you like to live in the city?" I asked, as I tried to scrape some of the icy muck off my boots with a stick.

"No," Maya said, staring at the faint outline of the high-rise buildings. "All that traffic and concrete? How would I care for my dogs?" I stared down at the ground.

Maya patted my knee. "I know you love the city. I help dogs, but I've never helped a little girl before. Give me time. I think I can reunite you with your mother."

I sighed and pushed some strands of hair out of my eyes. "Maybe Mom will call today. If they let you call from jail, if she is in jail."

"Try not to worry. Everything slows down during the holidays." Maya stood up, and all the dogs rose with her. I held tight to Nemo and Eightball. All of a sudden, Nemo began to tug on his leash and pull me down the trail. He was so strong. I could not stop him. Rather than let go, I found myself stumbling after him while Eightball happily picked up speed and followed along.

"Fiddle sticks," Maya said, "Nemo is heading back to the shelter. He does this when he gets homesick. My knees are bad. I won't be able to keep up with him."

"I'll hold on," I yelled back at her. "I'll stay with him."

She laughed. "He'll take you safely back to the shelter. See you in a few minutes." I half ran and half trotted as Nemo pulled me forward. I now was the one on a leash, not him. One thing was certain. Life was not dull with Maya. Mom seemed to be mistaken about the suburbs.

CHAPTER
TWELVE

When I got back to the shelter I was out of breath. Nemo plunked down next to me panting and dripping long ropes of drool. Only the giant pup Eightball seemed unaffected by our wild run. He spun in a mad circle chasing his tail, while Nemo pawed at the gate, trying to get back inside. I leaned against the chainlink fence and watched two men in orange parkas as they worked in the kennel area, emptying water dishes and filling bowls with kibble. Since they were strangers, I decided to wait for Maya before I went inside the gate. Nemo watched me calmly with bloodshot eyes. He seemed relieved to be home.

When Maya finally appeared with her tangle of dog leashes, I followed her to the kennels.

"Borgia, I want you to meet Bjorn." She nodded to a tall, blond-haired man with a reddish beard. He smiled, saluted, then turned and hurried away. "Bjorn is shy," Maya whispered. "He prefers dogs to people, but Mr. Will over there is very friendly. She had no sooner said this, than the other man in an orange parka approached us, smiling.

"Will, this is Borgia. Borgia, Mr. Will." Mr. Will pulled off a glove and extended a hand. He had sky blue eyes that crinkled with wrinkles. His whole face seemed to smile.

"Nice to meet you, Borgia, welcome to the world of dogs." Mr. Will talked so fast and said so much, I could barely keep track of what he was saying. He just kept talking, barely pausing. "Yessiree, there are a lot of dogs need homes, and we are looking for just the right match."

"Will, Borgia isn't picking out a dog. She's staying with me for a while." Maya set three dogs free into the fenced area back of the shelter.

"Alrighty then," said Mr. Will. "That's even better. You can be a friend to all the dogs, and while you're at it, come on over and meet my son Remy. Good golly, he could use some company during this long snowbound vacation."

Maya interrupted Mr. Will and looked down at me. "Borgia, Mr. Will loves rock music. What is the name of your mother's band?"

"He won't know it," I said. "Almost no one has heard of it."

"Try me," Mr. Will said, holding his chin in his hand. He laughed and tipped his head as if waiting for a challenge.

"Tides Out," I said, sure he not recognize it.

"Let's see," Mr. Will rubbed his hands together and held up his left index finger. "I believe I know that band. Tides Out, ah Tides Out. First, they released an EP. Came out end of summer couple years ago. Only three songs, but it got some play on the college stations." He paused, touched his forehead as if the details suddenly became clear. "That was kinda the little bump they needed. The next album was pretty complete. Strong. Catchy."

I could not keep track of all Mr. Will was saying. I tried not to yawn. I knew yawning was rude. Maya looked at me sympathetically, as she worked to untangle the leashes.

"You can tell Mr. Will loves music and knows a lot about it."

Mr. Will was still talking, ignoring Maya. "Got it, got it--just came to me." He tapped his head. "The lead guitar player is Del Olsen, and the female vocalist is Claire, no Celia, Celia Harringa." He pointed his finger at me and lifted his chin proudly.

"Celia is my mom," I said, amazed. Mr. Will knew my mom's name. In one fell swoop, I liked him. This man knew my mother. "Do you live in Seattle?" I asked hopefully. Phil's brow furrowed. He scratched his head.

"No, no, I live right down that forest path over there. You can follow the road, but I prefer the trails through the woods, natural soft underfoot, mostly old bark, pine needles layers. Of course, now the snow has buried...."

Maya interrupted him again without turning around. She was busy hanging up the leashes. "Borgia's mother told her people on the Eastside are boring." I tensed, expecting some critical response, but Mr. Will just laughed.

"May be true," he said. "I know how your mom feels. Sometimes you just have to be in the city, experience the bright lights, the noise, all the cars. Lots of good music in the city, can't get enough. Restaurants are great too, little hole in the wall places, delicious food from all over the world."

I wondered if anything bothered Mr. Will—obviously not the barking dogs or all the poop he was hosing down in the cages.

"You work here?" I asked.

"Yep," he continued to spray the concrete floor with a stiff wand of water.

"Mr. Will volunteers," Maya interjected. "He donates his time."

"I have another job to bring in the bacon," Mr. Will added.

"The bacon?"

"The money." He chuckled and rubbed his hands together

as if he had made a funny joke. "I work on my computer from home."

"Folks like Mr. Will help to keep the shelter open," Maya said. "His work is a donation investment from his heart. A true volunteer."

"Heh, Heh," Mr. Will nodded. "That's right. That's right."

Maya waved goodbye with her head as she held two small dogs, one in each arm. Mr. Will continued to talk. "Got to run, see you later."

THIRTEEN

"Sometimes it's hard to get away from Mr. Will," Maya confided as we stepped onto the back porch and pulled off our muddy shoes. She opened the screen door and set the two little dogs on the floor. They immediately ran down the hall and disappeared through the flip flop. "You need an escape plan. Mr. Will can talk all day."

"I like him. He knows my mom."

"Right, your mom." Maya's eyes narrowed. "We can form a plan." She opened a cupboard and pushed around some boxes and tins. "Where did I put that canister of cookies? Do you like tea?"

"I don't know much about tea. I tried coffee twice."

Maya smiled. "Teatime will be extra special today–break out the china, the silver spoons and especially the tea cozy."

"Tea cozy?" Maya held up what appeared to be a rag doll with a bright quilted skirt.

"You place the cozy on top of the teapot to retain the heat, keep the tea hot." She set a kettle on the stove and bustled about the kitchen. " We must dress up for a tea party. Gloves, yes?"

"Sure!"

"And jewelry?" Maya added. "I have colored pearls–pink, orange and blue."

"Orange would match my Esmeralda costume," I said, forgetting that my Esmeralda costume had been ripped and shredded by puppy teeth when I first arrived at the shelter.

" Hats too," Maya added, as she plucked four floppy hats from pegs in the hall and laid them on the table.

"I have a princess crown in my suitcase." I ran upstairs, while Maya rummaged around in her bedroom searching for gloves. When I cracked open my wicker suitcase, I discovered my beloved Space Needle snow globe. I unwrapped it carefully and set it next to the shiny black Eightball on the nightstand. Both were round and needed to be shaken. Next, I set the princess crown on my head and paused for a moment in front of the mirror. The diamonds sparkled as if they were real jewels.

"Borgia, fleet of foot," Maya said after I flew down the stairs. "What a sparkly tiara. You look like a real princess."

Maya bustled about, making sandwiches, while I pulled on a pair of white gloves that reached up to my armpits. I lay out her china cups and saucers while she fussed with a velvet pillbox hat, smoothing its wrinkled veil. Finally, she handed me a plate stacked with miniature sandwiches, little squares of cucumbers with peanut butter, and egg salad with celery.

"Are those potato chips in the sandwiches?" I asked, pulling back a square of bread.

Maya laughed. "You caught me! Potato chip sandwiches are my weakness, but most of this food is healthy. If we eat healthy, we can have a little clotted cream. See if you can find the glass mixing bowl for me in that lower cupboard, while I set up the electric mixer."

I bent over and dug in the crowded cupboard, struggling to move a stack of pie plates, while wearing gloves. Finally, I uncovered the big glass mixing bowl. As I lifted the bowl, a furry brown face with whiskers popped up over the rim.

"Mouse!" I screamed. Fortunately, Maya reached out and grabbed the bowl just as I recoiled in horror, nearly dropping it.

"Not a mouse," she said, setting the bowl in the sink. "It's only Hurry Harry, the hamster. An escape artist. I can't keep him in a cage. Oh, for heavens sakes, Hurry." Maya looked exasperated as the hamster scampered up her arm, then down her leg and across the floor. "He prefers life in a glass bowl to life in a wire cage."

Maya managed to grab the little creature by the scruff of his neck and dangle him over to me. His nose was twitching, and his little black whiskers tickled my hand. His cheeks were incredibly fat and swollen. "Cheeks are stuffed full of food," Maya said as she shifted the scrambling animal from one hand to another, trying to contain him.

She dropped Hurry into a metal cage hidden under the coats in the back hall and secured the latch. Hurry emptied his cheeks, pushing sunflower seeds, potato chips and bits of dog kibble out in a pile on the sawdust. Then he began to run madly round and round on a wire wheel going nowhere.

"At least for a brief time we can see him," Maya said, running the beaters on her mixer in a clean, hamster-free bowl. She handed me a rubber scraper covered in white.

"Whipped cream, just like on my hot chocolate."

Maya smiled and poured a stream of golden tea into china cups covered in yellow and pink flowers. She tucked me into her cozy kitchen nook seat with a view out the window to the pasture—one of the few rooms where dogs were not allowed. Greet, however, the great puff ball of a cat, jumped up on the bench next to Maya and purred.

" Greet likes tea parties." She removed her china saucer and poured him some cream. Greet lapped it up with a dainty pink tongue.

"Look! That's the white wolf that frightened Mannie," I pointed a gloved finger out the window to the pasture.

Maya didn't look as she lifted her veil and took a bite of shortbread. "Halo, the Great Pyrenees, is a dog, not a wolf. He prefers to be in the field. I'm glad the snow has mostly melted. I don't like to leave him outside in bad weather."

"Won't he harm those goats and sheep?"

Maya smiled. "Those sheep and goats are his family. Halo wants to protect them. That's what Great Pyrenees do best. Now tell me, who is Mannie?"

I told her, and she seemed confused. "Okay, I need to hear more, Borgia."

I tried to explain, but Maya just seemed to become more and more puzzled.

"You have never gone to school. You don't know your birthday." She took off her pillbox hat and ran her hands through her thick hair. "It doesn't make sense. We have to figure out the next step." Just as she said that, there was a crash as if glass was breaking in her bedroom.

Maya jumped up and ran down the hall to her bedroom where Greet had knocked some photos on the floor. As I followed Maya, I noticed her walls were painted a light shade of lavender.

"Is purple your favorite color?" The curtains were patterned with purple lilies, even the bedspread was purple. Maya told me her school colors were purple and gold.

"For the University of Washington?" The UW campus was not far from our houseboat, so I saw the purple and gold school colors often, especially on game days when the fans all wore purple and gold.

Maya nodded. "Do you know the mascot?"

"Dogs."

"Yes, the Huskies. One dog I have never had dropped off here." Maya laughed. I did too. It felt good.

"Glass everywhere," she said, getting more serious as she stared down at the foot of her bed. "Be careful where you step." She glanced at the haughty cat walking up and down on her bed, sinking his claws into the quilted comforter. "Stop it, Greet!" She tried to catch him, but he leapt to the floor and strode out of the room, ignoring her.

"Your family?" I asked, picking up one of the framed pictures from the floor. The glass had cracked. Shards were strewn everywhere.

"Me with Mom and Dad." Maya pointed to the small red-haired girl tucked in between her parents.

"Are you an only child?"

"At that point I was. My sister was born when I was nine. An only child for nine years."

"No brothers?"

"Nope." Maya started carefully picking up pieces of glass and placing them in a dust bin.

"What's your sister's name?"

"Rose. I call her Rosy. Only half-sisters. Different fathers. My dad died when I was eight. Mom remarried. When they moved to Florida, I stayed behind to finish high school at Roosevelt. I never saw Rosy much after that. We finally got together when she returned to Seattle to attend college. Unfortunately, we had a falling out. We haven't spoken in years. Sadly, we lost track of one another."

"Oh," I said, as I picked up another picture. The glass on this photo was also shattered. Two young girls stared out from the photograph, one obviously a teenager, the other a little girl sitting on a tricycle. Both girls had auburn hair that looked burnished bronze. Something about the older girl caught my eye. It must be Maya. So pretty, so slender. There were no owl glasses hiding her green eyes. "I have a pin like that one you are wearing," I said, pointing to the collar of her blouse. "It's golden, too."

Maya peered at the photo. "Oh, the golden spur. Received it sophomore year when I was inducted into Honor Society. You have a golden spur pin? Did your mom attend Roosevelt High School?"

"I don't think so, but Mom never talks about school."

"We need to figure out why your mother had you dropped off here. There must be some connection." I shrugged my shoulders, but at that moment, a seed was planted in my mind. My mom must know Maya. Maya must know my mom. There was something she was not telling me. I could sense it. Maya said we would take the next few days to figure out a plan. She would not call the police. I breathed a sigh of relief.

FOURTEEN

Every morning I helped Maya fill the water bowls and hose down the kennels. Then we hooked leashes to a few select dogs and headed out for a walk. As the dogs pulled us forward, Maya asked me questions. One morning as we were returning from our walk, I noticed a big brown UPS truck parked out front. Mr. Will was facing the truck, laughing and slapping his knees. Even though it was still rather cold outside, the UPS driver was dressed in brown shorts and green knee socks. He just nodded at Mr. Will and kept walking backwards, as if he needed to escape.

"We need to rescue that poor man," Maya said. She turned the dogs loose into the dog-runs and hurried over.

"A package," Maya said happily, looking at Mr. Will's hands. "My new dog tags, I bet."

Mr. Will smiled and waved goodbye to the UPS man, who had finally made it back and now sat behind the steering wheel of his truck. However, as Maya reached out for the thick manila envelope, Mr. Will retracted the package and said, "Not so fast, Maya, nope, not for you. Let's see. All righty, it says, Borgia,

Borgia of the, of the...." He paused and cocked his head toward me for help.

"Of-the-Glades," I said, as he handed over the package. I tore at the fat envelope, ripping it open, hoping it was from Mom. I pulled out a handwritten note.

The note read, Dear Borgia, Here is your phone. Charged it, but you need to buy a charger. Hope you are OK. Harlo.

I dumped out the familiar cell phone with its distinctive purple cover with silver streaks. It was Mom's phone, the one I left in Mannie's car on Christmas Eve. The battery icon glowed green, fully charged. Maya nodded approvingly.

"Progress," she said, right before I disappeared. I grabbed the phone and ran to the house, tore up the back stairs to my room and flopped on the bed. I wanted to be alone. Only Eight-ball had followed me. He sat very quiet and rested his nose on the bedspread as if he sensed my apprehension.

I typed in Mom's password, "Rockstar" and the phone clicked open. There were no recent phone calls. Harlo must have cleared the call history. Happily, there were three texts to me—one from the day after Christmas and two from yesterday. I clicked on the first one and held my breath. The messages were from Mom.

Just got out of jail

Police kept us overnight

Confiscated my meds

No child or missing jewelry

Released this AM. So wrong!

Back ASAP

Do not call the police

I felt my heart drop a little. Back ASAP? Where was she? I read the text again, my mind spinning. Missing jewelry? I was the one missing, the one left behind. Mom had very little jewelry, mostly homemade bracelets she crafted from shells and glass beads. I opened the second text message:

I am OK but rattled
Emergency plan.
Gone to Canada
To finalize Paris deal
Plus practice
Borgia, stay at the shelter
OMG France and Paris
No calls from Canada
No phone plan. Love Mom.
Do not call the police!

I quickly texted back.

Just got your phone back
Come get me
Why did you leave me
Why Canada
Do you know Maya
What phone are you using
Love Borgia

A MESSAGE immediately flashed in red.
FAILURE UNABLE
TO DELIVER
My heart sank. I felt incredibly depressed. Mom was safe, but she had left me. It didn't make sense. How did she know I was going to be OK? Why a dog shelter? Why Maya?

I found Maya resting in her lounge chair, sipping a cup of cinnamon spice tea, surrounded by attentive dogs. Greet sat on top of the piano examining a paw, his claws extended.

"I can't wait to hear," Maya said. "Tell me everything." I read Mom's texts out loud. Maya looked even more perturbed. She asked if she could examine Mom's phone. I handed it off to her and slumped on the sofa. A fluff ball dog immediately jumped into my lap.

After Maya examined Mom's phone, she suddenly quit asking me questions about my life. She seemed to accept that Mom would eventually come back to retrieve me. In the meantime, she had some ground rules for me to follow. I suspected Maya knew more about my mom than she was telling me, but I was so used to being the only kid in a group of adults who kept me in the dark, I just accepted my mysterious circumstances.

On a positive note, Mom had contacted me. I knew where she was. Apparently, she had planned to dump me off at this dog shelter. On a negative note, Mom left for Canada and I had no way to contact her while she was there. I missed her and Del too.

Maya said I could stay with her as long as I wanted. For some reason, she no longer talked about contacting the police or trying to figure out where I should go. Her main focus now seemed to be setting up a schedule for me to follow. I was not used to plans that centered around me.

"Borgia, if you stay much longer, you have to go to school, real school, and get a sound public education. I don't have the knowledge or energy to home school you."

At first I was alarmed by the idea, but secretly, I had always wanted to attend school. Mom might come and get me before I had to attend school, anyway.

"I don't have any records," I said. "Mom said public schools require lots of identification, kind of like a dog license."

"I have a solution," Maya said. "The school counselors check all the records. We don't want them to be alarmed. How about I tell them I am your aunt? Aunt Maya?" She held her folded hands up like she was saying a little prayer, like I wouldn't possibly go along with it.

At first her words struck me as fishy. I was supposed to tell people, Maya, the owl-eyed owner of a dog shelter, was my aunt? Sounded crazy, but the more I thought about it, the more I warmed to the idea. "Aunt Maya" had a nice ring. It also reminded me to conduct some detective work, to find out how Maya was connected to Mom.

Maya had a business office stuffed with albums and a desk full of folders. In the hope of discovering some clues, I decided to investigate—become a kid detective. Mom said she had no family, except me. Many times, I annoyed her by asking if I had a brother or sister somewhere. It never occurred to me to ask if I had an aunt. Aunt Maya?

"School requires information on each student," Maya announced. "We can say your records are coming but not yet available. If the school administration thinks I am your aunt, a legal guardian, there won't be as many roadblocks to getting you admitted and on your way to becoming a matriculated student. One of the school secretaries also owes me a favor. I gave her a dog."

"Got it, Aunt Maya." She placed her hand over her mouth in surprise at the sound of the two words together. We both laughed.

CHAPTER

FIFTEEN

The cold, rainy days dripped by, often drumming on the roof as if Mannie were up there banging away on his drums. Bump, bump, pitter, patter, thrum, thrum. Grey days often surprised with partial sun breaks that burst through the clouds. When the sun dropped in for a visit, it could be blinding. Seattle rain dwellers could barely stand such brightness—squinting, complaining of headaches from all the light. Del, who grew up in sunny Alberta, Canada, called Seattleites mole people. Maya laughed at the expression when I used it. I had to admit, I was more comfortable in the rain. In my current world it was raining dogs. Each new day at the shelter brought hours crammed full of canines—wagging tails, muddy paws, clouds of hair, slobbering and barks.

Like clockwork, every morning I checked my phone to see if Mom had left a message. I carried her cell phone everywhere, hoping to feel that familiar vibration that would reconnect me to my old life.

Christmas vacation was almost over, and a brand-new year set to begin. Maya said she had registered me at Arrowridge Elementary School, a fifteen-minute walk downhill. Arrowridge sat in a clearing surrounded by native forest, mostly Douglas fir and cedar trees. The idea of attending school was both thrilling and terrifying.

Thankfully, my life at the shelter felt safe, even secure. Eightball slept in my room and followed me around during the day. He liked to fetch sticks–the bigger the better–and he loved to eat whatever I was eating, carrots, celery, even apple peels. He was the biggest pup Maya had ever seen. She showed me how to train him, using treats. Soon I taught him to shake hands, roll over and stay. He already knew how to fetch.

One morning while I was throwing sticks for Eightball, Maya called Arrowridge Elementary on her landline telephone and spoke to the main office secretary, Erma Pearson. Maya told Erma she was worried about my lack of records. The secretary was eager to help. Maya had found Erma a rescue pup, her little mop of a dog, Polly. She spent every school day under Erma's desk in the main office, so Erma was eager to repay a favor. She knew all the pathways to register me as a temporary student. She also instructed Maya how to fill out the requisite forms and check the school website for upcoming events.

Maya announced that the first day back from winter break, Arrowridge was hosting a winter carnival. This event included a house plant show, with local gardeners on hand to judge and award prizes. Also, a first ever "Famous Painting Day," was taking place. Every student was encouraged to come dressed in costume as a person or creature connected to a famous painting. Maya loved the idea but was puzzled on how to proceed.

"What painting would you like to be?" she asked me as she whisked some eggs in a bowl.

"I don't know." I was busy spreading Maya's homemade jam on a piece of toast and trying to play a game on my phone, with sticky fingers. "Do I have to participate in the Winter Carnival?"

"No." Maya flipped the eggs, now bubbling and popping in the fry pan. " Might be fun. Consider the possibilities before you make up your mind."

Mom had a copy of *The Scream* painting on the wall of the houseboat, a distorted person with their mouth in a shrill "Oh no." Del had decorated his apartment with black velvet paintings, mostly rock musicians that glowed in the dark.

"Wait. I've got it." I set my glass of milk down so hard it sloshed out on the table. "Whoops," I grabbed some paper towels to sop it up. "The girl left behind, the one with her hair blowing, standing on the edge of a cliff in your jigsaw puzzle."

Maya waved her spatula through the air as if she were performing a magic trick. "Yes, that's the ticket. Why didn't I think of that, the wonderful Eastman Johnson painting."

Every time I looked at the completed puzzle still sitting on the card table in the living room, I strongly identified with the girl and her blowing hair. The girl left behind—waiting, waiting, waiting, just like me.

"I can recreate her dress," Maya exclaimed. "I design my own patterns." I didn't know what to say. My experience with sewing brought back gross images of Volly's stern face and knitting needle hairdo, but I held my tongue.

Unfortunately, during the costume design, I became a living mannequin. Maya turned me round and round on a needlepoint footstool and insisted I stand perfectly still while an assortment of crazed dogs barked and romped on the carpet below. A recent arrival to the shelter, a little white and brown Corgi mix, ran in circles round the basset Deville, who threw back her head and bayed, hoping to get a treat. A Jack Russell leapt in the air, snapping at the yardage. It was like a crazy circus that Maya was able to ignore. The longer I tried to stand still, the more cranky I felt. I blamed the dogs.

Meanwhile Maya, her mouth full of pins, critically studied

the black velvet fabric draped over me. She pondered, then leaned over the card table and held a magnifying glass up to study the girl in the puzzle, still missing the one piece the bassett Deville had swallowed.

"I can make your hair appear to blow," Maya said, as she twisted my hair into a knot. "Homemade honey meringue. Will seem just like a stiff Nor'easter took hold of it."

My hair was now back to its natural straw color–ironically the same color as the girl's hair in the painting. My dark Esmeralda hair had long faded—the black dye washed down the drain. That afternoon as I posed for Maya, a cramp struck my leg, making it more and more difficult to hold still. Sometimes a pin stuck me and I jumped.

I was so used to my readymade clothes. I was not convinced a homemade costume would work. However, gradually, as the new costume emerged, it forced me to picture a new version of myself. I felt strange but hopeful. Little twinges of sadness sometimes pricked the hope, popping my confidence, but most of the time I saw a new era beginning to take shape with Maya guiding the way.

"Your painting choice will be epic," she said, mumbling through her pins as she rummaged through lopsided bolts of cloth. She picked up a deep red velvet, then set it down and held up a bolt of black wool.

"Wool is better than velvet. A Seattle cloak needs to be warm for winter and practical in rain." Once again, she was talking out loud and humming to herself. "I wonder if the girl is holding a hand warming muff. I could fashion one out of an old mink stole."

"The girl is holding books, remember? Also, I see a hat pressed up against her dress." I was not feeling charitable. My legs ached. Pinpricks of depression stabbed my heart, and venomous thoughts ran through my mind.

"A hat," Maya said skeptically. "I can't see it."

Exactly, I wanted to say, because you are practically blind, but I bit my tongue instead. Today Maya's thick glasses especially made her look like a ruffled owl. The pugs looked ugly, panting and snorting through their smashed faces. Nemo and Mobley were disgusting. Ropes of drool dangled from their jowls. Also the room smelled strongly of dogs. I wanted to pinch my nose, but I was supposed to stand still.

"We need peace and quiet," Maya muttered, still talking through her pins as if she could read my mind. She padded over to her remote and flipped on the cat channel to distract the dogs, but meowing TV cats were just as annoying. As I watched, Maya leaned over the puzzle, pulling out pieces to examine more closely. Meanwhile, the little dogs stormed the TV, leaping at the cats.

"Maya, can I sit down please? I feel lightheaded."

"Oh, sorry," Maya said. "Two more minutes, I promise. Here, have a drink of water. I want to do my best work. The counselor said most students will participate. I read it can be any painting, so, so, so...." She continued to mutter, her words clipped and random. I sighed. I wanted to go to school, but I already knew how to read. I could do my multiplication and use a computer. Still, I did not know anything about the social world of children. Most of my life had been spent with adults. With anxiety over the new school, I was growing more and more cranky. As if that were not enough, all the animals were getting on my nerves.

"Maya," I screamed. "Look!" I pointed to the wall. Greet strode haughtily along the catwalk, with the hamster, Hurry Harry, dangling from his mouth by the scruff of his neck. Hurry was obviously still very much alive, his eyes bright and black. His two little hands neatly folded in front of him as if he thought Greet was giving him free public transport from one spot to another.

"Greet!" Maya screamed. She grabbed her yardstick and batted the cat. As the stick came toward Greet, he froze, a grey paw poised in midair. Then he dropped Hurry and performed an amazing cat flip on the narrow ledge and ran down the catwalk. Hurry Harry scurried along the ledge in the opposite direction, dropped onto the piano and sped over the black and white keys, disappearing into a large houseplant with wide green leaves. Maya exhaled and fell back in her recliner. The electronic motor whirred as the chair tipped all the way back. Dogs ran to the wall, barking hysterically. The pins had flown out of Maya's mouth onto the table and floor. I quickly knelt and picked them up before the dogs could eat them. The fabric wrapped around me fell away into a pile. I set it on the table and walked away.

Really, all these animals were a great deal of trouble. At least school would give me a break from all the commotion at the shelter. As the afternoon wore on, my nerves frayed even more. The stress of such a big undertaking rankled me. Unfortunately, more and more, I took it out on Maya by complaining.

CHAPTER
SIXTEEN

The next morning, I felt especially grumpy. Eightball woke me twice in the night, chewing on his squeaky toy, then tugging on my covers. As I watched Maya madly scrub an encrusted fry pan, I announced, "I don't like dogs." The words stuck in my throat the moment I said them. I set my chin and furiously stirred my cereal round and round, without looking up to see her reaction. Rain pounded on the roof and gutters. Water streamed down the windows. By now my corn flakes were soggy. I didn't feel like eating. I didn't feel like doing anything.

"What's the matter, Borgia?" Maya asked, clattering dirty bowls in the sink. I didn't want to say, I am worried about school, so I used the dogs as an excuse.

"I planned to enter the houseplant contest, but Crumpet peed on the orchid in my room last night."

"What, where is it?" Maya turned to look at me.

"I set the pot on the floor to catch the sun. When I woke up, it was wilted and had dropped all its blossoms." I lifted my spoon, dripping with milk, and watched it stain my napkin.

Maya immersed her hands in soapy water. The splash of wet dishes and suds got louder, but she said nothing.

"A pug snuck into the kitchen and ate the last cupcake. Then it jumped on the table and licked the cube of butter." I studied Maya, who was still not responding. All the time I was talking, I realized that I sounded just like my mother, complaining about small things. I kept going anyway.

"I can't sit down without getting dog hair on my clothes. The little dogs won't let me watch TV. They bark at every animal that appears on the screen, even fish. Look how the Labradors patrol the bird feeder. The poor little birds can't eat any seed. Someone lunges at them whenever they land."

Still no response, so I hit as hard as I could. "I hate dogs," I yelled, as if trying to convince myself. "They bark all the time. They let terrible smells and chew up the sofa pillows. I think you should get rid of all of them." Of course, I could never part with Eightball. He was my pup. I started to sweat. I knew I was being impossible. I expected Maya to argue with me the way Mom would have, maybe even yell or explode. Instead, there were just more clinks of plates and splashing dishwater.

I felt frozen. I knew I had hurt Maya. It felt terrible, as if the cold in the rainy day had entered my soul and struck out all the sunlight. I didn't know what to do. All the incidents I recounted were true, but I didn't care. Part of me wanted to run and throw my arms around her, but instead I sprang up, slammed my chair against the table and stormed upstairs to my room.

I felt traitorous and evil. If I were a dog, I would probably bite someone for no reason at all. A muzzle would be fastened over my face, and I'd be locked in a cage until I settled down. I sat by the window staring at the rain. "Boring," I said out loud, and my eyes blurred with tears. What was Mom doing? Was Canada full of rain too? She had mentioned her upcoming Paris trip, but not with me along too. I imagined strolling across a bridge in Paris and climbing the Eiffel tower. "No dogs allowed," I whispered. "Good." Then I had a revelation. My mother got rid of me. Maybe I was just trouble, like these bothersome dogs.

A knock sounded on the door, and Maya entered, carrying a small clay pot with a spiky green plant. "You're right to be upset. I think you should take this plant to the flower show instead of the orchid."

"It doesn't have any flowers." The plant was downright ugly.

"No flowers, but it has these spiky leaves. It's a Venus Flytrap. Besides getting food from the sun, it catches flies and small insects."

"Maya?" I said, taking the strange potted plant out of her hands.

"Yes."

"I'm sorry for what I said about the dogs. I don't hate them. Sometimes they make me angry." I set the Venus Flytrap on a high bookshelf where it would be out of their reach.

"I know, dear. Animals are frustrating. They take a lot of work and patience. Sometimes I hate them, too."

"You do?" I sat back down on the edge of my bed.

"Maybe not hate, but it can feel like hate. Then I remember all the wonderful qualities dogs possess, and I forgive them."

"Do you think my mother thought I was too much trouble?"

Maya took off her glasses and sank down next to me. "I think your mother loves you more than anyone. Her life got complicated and out of control. I am so happy you are here. You are a great comfort to me."

"Really?" I fidgeted and swung my stocking feet.

"Really." Maya looked at me without her round glasses. Her eyes were not so big. She did not look like an owl.

"More comfort than the dogs?" I asked, fishing shamelessly for a compliment.

Maya laughed. "You are way more comforting than the dogs. You don't pee on the curtains and bark at the TV."

"But I'm mean. That's worse."

Maya shook her head. "All your faults are like this." She held up her finger and thumb to indicate a teeny bit, "but your good traits fill the room. You are frustrated, Borgia. You feel hurt—all part of being human. There is a price for change, but in the long run, hopefully some of the new parts will be for the better."

"Like meeting you," I said kindly, "like finding Eightball."

"Exactly. Maybe the suburbs are not as bad as your mom said."

I rolled my eyes, thinking back to my rude comments when I first arrived. Maya gave me a big hug. I hugged her back.

CHAPTER

SEVENTEEN

wo days later, I attended my first ever day of public school. It felt a bit strange to be dressed up as someone else, but I always loved costumes, especially my Esmeralda outfit. Now, I represented an old fashioned girl in a famous piece of art. My hair stuck straight out, as if caught in a fierce wind. The girl in the Eastman Johnson painting stood on the edge of a high cliff. I stood on a forested hill, ready to set out with Maya and four dogs on my way to Arrowridge Elementary. Now public school, for me, Borgia, a girl who had never set foot in a classroom. As I crunched down the snowy path, Maya walked ahead in her quilted parka, a lavender scarf wrapped about her face. Her grey and white wool socks were neatly folded over the edge of her boots, as she pulled the sled behind her.

"Your new school is at the bottom of the hill," she said, pointing a thick mitten toward a clearing where an older two-story building stood, surrounded by newer one-story structures. The elaborate maze of playground equipment looked especially appealing to me.

"I thought it would be fun to zoom down the hill on the

sled, but now I wonder." Maya gazed skeptically down the icy path.

I was worried about risking my fancy costume on the sled, but Maya encouraged me, so I lowered myself down behind her. Then she dropped the dog leashes, and we took off. I blinked as the freezing air whizzed by stinging my face. Maya expertly guided the sled, avoiding the tall, crusted trees and lumps that often meant rocks or stumps. The dogs ran joyfully behind us, barking all the way. At the base of the hill, she gathered all the dog leads together, and the excited canines looked up at her expectantly for more fun.

"This afternoon, I'll bring the big dogs to pull us up the hill, or we can walk. I am not fond of steep hills. They bother my knees." Maya smoothed out my costume and sprayed my stiff hair one last time. She often limped after our walks on the trails. It dawned on me now what a grand effort she was making for me.

"The snow is melting. The weather is changing," she continued, " and dogs are not allowed in the school yard. I will wait here until you check in at the main office, that door with a narrow window." I nodded. "Now remember, my friend Erma is the head secretary. She's expecting you."

"OK," I said, gritting my teeth.

Maya pretended not to notice my anxiety. "Look, dripping icicles on the playground equipment. Definitely heating up."

I was not warming up at all. My emotions were bunched in a tight little knot, like hundreds of rubber bands wound into a ball. I did not smile. I did not frown. I felt like the giant snow-covered boulders, hard and cold. I stepped through the opening in the school fence and took tentative steps across the play-ground, staring down at my high-button shoes. Maya had discovered the crumpled pair at the bottom of a box in Value Village. "Only $2.99," she said happily, as if she had discovered buried treasure. They were not good snow shoes. Fortunately, the walks had been de-iced. The sound of my feet, tapping along closer and closer to school, sounded scary, definitely unreal and hollow.

I pulled open the metal door labeled MAIN OFFICE. Two office secretaries sat behind the counter. Both looked up from their computers at the same time.

"Wonderful costume," the secretary in a blue sweater said, "but what artist painted you? Don't tell me. Let me think."

The taller secretary, with dark hair, and silver bracelets on her tan wrists, leaned over and conversed with the blue sweater lady in a hushed voice. "Winslow Homer?" she said, raising her eyebrows and gazing at me over her glasses.

"Nope." I shook my head.

"Wait, one more guess." The lady in the blue sweater held up her hand as if to stop me from speaking. "John Singer Sargent?" She looked at me hopefully, her blue eyes glowing. I shook my head again.

"All right, enough of this guessing game," the lady with the bracelets said, staring at her computer screen. "We need to get you registered. What is your name?"

" Borgia OftheGlades, my Aunt Maya already...." I was interrupted before I could finish.

"Oh, Borgia, you are already registered." The lady in the blue sweater talked while she clicked away on her computer keys. "We have been expecting you. Love your Aunt Maya. She gave me my little Dolly Polly sleeping under my desk here." She pointed down at her feet and smiled as if we now shared a secret. "Welcome to Arrowridge. I'm Erma. Your aunt's friend."

I tried to smile, but my face felt paralyzed.

"Is OftheGlades one word?" the lady with dark hair asked.

'Yes," I said, squirming uneasily, wondering what she would ask next.

"I already registered Borgia online," Erma announced.

"Found you," the dark-haired lady peered at her computer screen, beginning to type and talk at the same time. "Pronounce your last name one more time." Her printer hummed to life, and she handed me a registration card. "Give this to your teacher."

Erma paused, her fingers poised on the computer keys. "Your Aunt Maya is wonderful, performs such public service."

"I'm Layla," the dark-haired lady added. "Just so you know, Erma and I run the school."

Both ladies giggled. "It's true. We are in charge, secretly, of course."

Erma pretended to whisper. "If you ever need anything, we are here to help, but just between the two of us, we allow Mr. Oakley to think he is in charge, because, well, he is the principal."

"Our fearless leader," Layla said, smiling and pointing to the words "Principal Oakley"on the door. She stared at her computer and continued to tap the keyboard. I admired her long fingernails. "Your classroom is 204. Go out the door, turn right and enter the old brick building with the bell tower. Take the oak staircase. Your room is the first one, on the left at the top of the stairs. My favorite room in the whole school by the way. Wonderful view from the windows."

"Do you want me to come and show you?" Erma asked. Three more students had filed into the office. One was accompanied by parents. They had formed a line and were waiting for help.

"No," I said, immediately regretting it. I wished I had said yes, but it was too late. I turned and looked out the window to the edge of the woods where Maya still stood. The dogs strained at their leashes whenever a student passed by. Slipping out the door, I did not wave or acknowledge her, but the dogs barked when they saw me and wagged their tails.

"Those your dogs?" a sandy haired boy covered in green leaves asked. All the dogs were barking. Maya was waving.

"No," I said rudely, and walked past him without making eye contact.

"Crazy hair," another boy commented, grinning as I paused on the sidewalk. He was dressed like a pirate. "What painting are you?" Two more kids were staring at me, but then they were staring at everybody.

"*The Girl I left behind*," I snapped, not giving the complete name of the painting.

"Never heard of it, but I have never heard of most paintings." He shrugged and smiled good naturedly. "This contest was thought up by adults, not kids. Kinda boring, but my mom had fun making the costume."

"I'm Picasso," another boy announced, joining our group, "in his blue period." I looked at the boy's, blue face and hands. He walked on, and so did I.

I decided it was a good thing that everyone looked so strange and out of place. My hair stuck straight out as if the wind were blowing in a topsy turvy windstorm. As I followed two costumed kids into the brick building, there were children in weird costumes everywhere, like we had beamed down from some other planet. I headed up the staircase holding tight to the railing, following other students climbing the steps.

"Welcome, Borgia," my teacher said, as I stepped into the classroom and handed her my registration. She had clear, watery, blue eyes and tightly curled grey hair. Her white blouse was buttoned right up to the neck, with a silver cat pin on her collar. Her long skirt was perfectly pleated. I tried to speak but swallowed instead and looked around the class. The room had a row of paned windows along one side. Huge white boards and a big screen covered the front wall. The blowing radiator gave off a friendly scent of crayons and glue.

"Borgia, your desk is next to Kimberly." The teacher pointed a ruler at an empty desk in the very front.

I sat down next to a girl who was dressed as the Mona Lisa but with blond hair. On my right was a boy with black, slicked-back hair. He was dressed like a Native American with war paint on his cheeks.

"George Catlin painting," he said, pushing a feather out of his eyes. "I really am part Indian; I mean Native American. In my family, we still say Indian."

"I'm the cat in the hat," a skinny boy chimed in behind me. He kicked the back of my chair to get my attention. When I turned around, he reached up and squashed the red and white felt hat on his head and crossed his eyes. I couldn't help but smile.

"Stewart, I hate to tell you, but Dr. Seuss was not a painter." Kimberly shook her head disparagingly. "He was a children's author and illustrator."

"So,what?" Stewart said, frowning. "My costume is way cooler than yours, and I rhyme."

"It's not a competition," Kimberly whispered to me. "Well, maybe it is. There is a prize for the favorite, hopefully me." She was very matter of fact and seemed to believe she knew all the answers, unlike our classmates.

One of the students rolled a cart down the aisle and placed a laptop computer on every desk. The teacher reached down to touch my strange hairdo, then drew her hand back rather abruptly.

"Honey meringue spray," I said. "Aunt Maya made the sticky spray herself and calls it 'Bees flying.'" I made the name up on the spot and smiled. I hoped to impress the teacher with my knowledge, even if it was a bit fake.

"I see," my teacher raised her eyebrows skeptically. "How creative." At the same time, she pushed down on the antibacterial hand dispenser on her desk and rubbed her hands together. I was getting too hot in my black wool coat–what Maya referred to as a cloak–so I hung it over the back of my chair. Then I stared up at the giant wall map of the United States now featured on the front screen. I picked out my favorite states by their shapes: California, Idaho and Florida. I did not look at the other children behind me until we all had to say our names. Mrs. Dimelroot wanted to get to know us. Apparently she was new to the class, just like me.

When it was my turn, I stood up and turned to face the class. My cheeks felt hot. I'm sure they were flushed red. "My name is Borgia OftheGlades," I said. "My mother named me after a song she wrote." I made up that story about the origin of my name long ago, to answer all the questions adults asked about my strange last name. Then I added, "My mom is a rock musician." That part was true. I still did not look at the other children. I looked over their heads at the back of the room. Mom told me that's what she did when performing, if she felt nervous.

"What glades are those, Borgia?" my teacher asked.

"I think I know," the cat in the hat boy blurted out, waving his hand frantically. "The ones with crocodiles and sharp teeth, right? Like this." He made a motion with his arms. "Large jaws that snap if you get too close. I've been to the Everglades. You have to watch your feet for crocodiles lurking about. Never wear white shoes because the Crocs might think your shoes are marshmallows. Snap! Your foot is gone, just like that." He made the motion with his arms again and looked around to see if he was making an impression.

"You mean alligators, Stewart." Kimberly huffily corrected him, turning around in her chair. "The Everglades are in Florida. Alligators live in Florida, not crocodiles."

"Whatever!" Stewart stuck his tongue out at Kimberly. I felt confused.

Mom lived in Florida for a while. Was I born in the Everglades? Was that where she got my name? It bugged me to know so little about my past.

"Are you done, Borgia?" The teacher was staring at me. "Class, Borgia may want to tell us something else."

"No," I said. "I'm done," and I quickly sat down.

"Hmm," my teacher said as she walked up and down the rows of desks. "Yes, Kenny." She called on a boy dressed like a matador who raised his hand in the back row.

"I think Stewart means alligators," he said. "The Everglades are in Florida."

"Kenny, I just said that," Kimberly, blurted out. "You weren't paying attention." Kimberly looked completely annoyed. She swung her legs and tossed her long Mona Lisa hairdo. The matador boy looked hurt and put his head down on his desk.

"Nobody listens anymore," the boy dressed like an Indian whispered, leaning over to get my attention. He raised his eyebrows. "Mom says we all spend too much time on our phones and we...."

"Jim ,would you like to share what you are telling Borgia?" our teacher asked coldly. She crossed her arms and stood in front of his desk, tapping her foot.

Jim smiled ruefully and shook his head. "Sorry," he said, grimacing at me and drawing his finger across his neck as if she was about to cut off his head. When our teacher moved on down the aisle, Jim leaned back over and said, "I can draw some alligators for you. I'll look them up on my phone. I'm good at drawing."

Not long after that, a girl wearing a bright red shawl and a yellow skirt approached my desk. "I'm Frida Kahlo," she said, smiling. "Frida mostly painted herself, so I'm both a painting and a painter." She giggled. "Frida was Mexican, but I'm half Chinese. My Dad is Irish, but I look Chinese, right? Well, maybe not today. Do I look Mexican to you?"

"Yes," I said, studying her face.

"Not really," Kimberly announced, overhearing the conversation. "You look Asian."

"My name is Mei Ling," the girl said, ignoring Kimberly and leaning her elbows on my desk. "I am glad to have one more girl in our class. If you haven't noticed, there are way too many boys." Kimberly nodded in agreement, obviously listening to every word Mei Ling uttered.

I was not used to getting so much attention. Maya had told me school was about being in a room with a whole bunch of people and trying to get along. That seemed to be important and somewhat difficult, but I enjoyed the commotion. I was a bit surprised. After my introduction to the class, our teacher approached the white board and wrote her name in big blue letters.

"Now that we know the new student's name, here is mine. Repeat after me, students–Mrs. Dimelroot." We all said her name out loud together. "I am one of the school counselors, but I will be substituting in this class until your teacher, Mr. McNulty, returns from Canada." Oh no, this teacher was going to leave. I was just getting used to her. The rest of the morning, I felt a little nervous, knowing I still had to meet Mr. McNulty. Why was he in Canada anyway?

Fortunately, the day sped by at an alarming rate. By two-thirty when class dismissed, I had participated in an array of activities I had never before experienced. I sat in an all-school assembly. I sang two group songs. I marched in an all-school art gallery parade and was introduced to and shook hands with the school principal, Mr. Oakley, who already knew my name. He gave me a school t-shirt with the words "Arrowridge" in block white letters across the front, and a school pendant that featured our penguin mascot.

My Venus fly trap won a purple ribbon for most unusual house plant. Maya's *The Girl I Left Behind Me* costume took a large pink ribbon for most original and outstanding hairdo in a work of art. The prize was ice cream cones for everyone in my class or carrot sticks if your parents did not allow you to have sugar. Picasso's blue period painting took the grand prize of a vegetarian, gluten free pizza party for the entire class.

When a bell rang announcing the school day had ended, I was exhausted but eager to share my school experiences with Maya. The snow was almost completely melted, the weather warming. I walked back across the slushy school yard, happy to see Maya waiting outside the chain link fence, surrounded by a new assortment of dogs. As I stepped through the gap in the fence, the dogs squirmed and frolicked, licking me and batting me with their wet paws. The pugs tucked in their tails, cavorting and zooming in circles, finally leaping over the other dogs. I laughed. Maya wrapped her arms around me and gave me a big hug. She was more excited about my ribbons than I was. Nemo and Mobley pulled Maya uphill to the shelter. I preferred to walk, so the pugs hopped into Maya's lap for the free ride back.

CHAPTER
EIGHTEEN

During the next few weeks, I counted the days until Mrs. Dimelroot was going to be replaced. Twice she made me stay in during recess. One Friday after school, she called me up to her desk. I stared at the desktop covered with stacks of books and papers. She explained the messy part belonged to Mr. McNulty. The small, neat space marked off with blue tape was hers. This space was decorated with a brass letter D and a porcelain bear wearing a dress and a hat with flowers round the brim. A pencil and pen were laid out side by side next to a blank lined tablet with the heading 'Lila Dimelroot, School Counselor,' stamped on the top. A large plastic dispenser of purple hand sanitizer sat square in the middle. The strong antiseptic smell made my nose wrinkle.

Mr. McNulty's side was crowded with books and framed photographs. In one picture, a man was holding a fishing pole. Was that Mr. McNulty? In another photo a golden retriever practically smiled into the camera. There was also a mug full of highlighters, a multicolored rubric's cube and a box labeled "prizes". The messy section was much more interesting and made me remember how several of the kids had said they wished Mr. McNulty would hurry back. Right now, I wished he would, too.

One day Mrs. Dimelroot asked me to stay in from recess for the third time. "Borgia," she said, folding her hands together and resting them on her cleared desk space. "We don't pretend at school as much as you do. Facts are important, and standards need to be addressed. You need to focus on the real world in front of you, the world of education. I need you to concentrate, exert more effort, so you can complete the requisite curriculum and pass the state standardized tests."

"OK," I said, biting my cheek. Why did she think I was unfocused. Was it that, when people asked me about my name, I made up stories, mostly because I just didn't know the truth. Her words made me feel weak in the knees. I realized Mrs. Dimelroot did not approve of me. I did not like the vocabulary she often used or the sound of words like curriculum, better balance tests and pedagogy. I had no idea what she meant by state standards. The words were so dull. I tried not to yawn, but sometimes I could not help it.

"I don't like acronyms," I said, thinking Mrs. Dimelroot might agree. At least maybe she would approve that I used one of the vocabulary words she expected us to learn. Acronyms, as far as I understood, meant cramming a bunch of words together, capitalizing them and saving only the first letter. Acronyms tried too hard to draw attention to themselves while keeping their true identity secret, like bandits hiding behind bandanas and masks. The acronym STEM was a combination of the words: Science, Technology, Engineering and Math. There were so many confusing acronyms at school. I saw them as a bunch of capital letters stacked together for no good reason.

While I spoke, I noted the circles under Mrs. Dimelroot's eyes seemed to get even darker. I looked down at my feet. "As far as I can tell, acronyms are just secret code for a jumble of words. All you get is the first letter. You have to guess the rest of the letters."

As Mrs. Dimelroot listened, she began to type on her iPad. I wondered what she was writing about me. True, I knew one vocabulary word, but actually I was falling behind in class. I had barely started the thousand page workbook, *Spring into the Future*. The workbook made class seem twenty hours long. The pages were as thin and scratchy as the paper towels in the gas station restrooms I hated, and the workbook smelled of strange chemicals. It made me anxious just to look at the thick brick-like book. I had to fill in all the blank lines and every empty square box with writing on every single page. It was boring. I had difficulty finishing the sections we were assigned to complete each day. Often I had to miss part of recess to get caught up. Mrs. Dimelroot also regularly made me stay after school and work on my math.

At elementary school I did not get to choose what I wanted to study. I had a hard time focusing on oil derricks far out in the ocean or how the Romans engineered their roads thousands of years ago. There were so many numbers and instructions every-where, dividing up the day. Turn to this page. Check the bell. Watch the clock. Five minutes here, sixty minutes there. You had to keep track of all these minutes and move when the numbers on the clock told you. You could only eat lunch, use the bathroom and go outside at a very particular time. I hated that part. It seemed like we basically had to stay in our class-room all day, sitting at cramped little desks. I was not sure why numbers were so important. I did not really care about them, and I did not like being told when to move and when to sit still.

"So, let's start again," Mrs. Dimelroot was saying as she tapped her finger on her desk. "Try telling me some true facts about your life." I shifted my feet. I was standing with one foot on the other. I wanted to be successful. I wanted Mrs. Dimelroot to like me. I actually enjoyed being with all the students in my class. I put my finger to my lips and thought.

"Well," I said, trying to use a lot of numbers. "It is a fact, I live with twenty-two dogs, one human, one hamster, one cockatoo and a very bad cat. I also have my own dog named Eightball." There, I used some facts and numbers.

I tipped nervously while I stood on one foot but continued, "I have an Esmeralda costume that the pups chewed up. Aunt Maya plans to fix it." I made a point to put emphasis on the word 'Aunt.' "I own fourteen Barbies. One got her arm chewed off by a brindle bulldog named Slider." All this was true. I had not embellished any part. Being even more honest and reality based, I announced, "I live with Aunt Maya now, but only while my mom is traveling with her rock band."

I stared at the tight line of Mrs. Dimelroot's mouth. "Do you still play with dolls and dress up in your-what was it-a princess costume?" I wanted to tell her Esmeralda was not a princess, but I did not correct her.

"I have mostly outgrown my Esmeralda costume."

"Costumes are meant to be worn during special times," Mrs. Dimelroot said matter-of-factly, "like at our Winter Carnival."

"That's not true," I snapped. "My mom wears costumes all the time, and look, you are wearing a teacher costume right now."

"Excuse me," Mrs. Dimelroot smoothed her blouse. "These clothes are not a costume."

I shrugged. I knew it was pointless to argue with her. I decided to change the subject.

"I still have most of my Barbies. I never played with them much. Most of them go commando now."

"Commando?" Mrs. Dimelroot furrowed her brow as she scratched something on the yellow paper with a particularly beautiful ink pen marked with marble swirls.

"Naked," I said. "No clothes."

"Well I never," Mrs. Dimelroot blinked her piercing blue eyes, stuck both feet on the floor and scooted back in her rolling chair.

"That's a start," she said abruptly, apparently done asking me questions. Her pursed lips continued to make me uneasy, as if she actually thought it was a bad start, but she said I could go home. I did not have to stay and write in the giant workbook or fill in squares and boxes.

As I was leaving, I stopped in the hall to get a drink at the water fountain. While I was leaning over the porcelain basin, I overheard Mrs. Dimelroot talking about me in the next room. "Borgia has been isolated. She is odd, hasn't had a normal life. I am tempted to call Child Protective Services. She lives up at that animal shelter with that strange woman Maya and all those stray dogs."

My throat went dry. I let the water run back out of my mouth and down the drain. Child Protective Services would place me in foster care with complete strangers. Mom had warned me about that often enough.

The afterschool meeting with Mrs. Dimelroot made me more determined than ever to find out why Mom had me dropped off at an animal shelter. I sensed Maya had information about me she was not sharing. Since I had been unable to contact Mom, I decided to figure it out on my own. Maya had a small office full of folders and records. I hoped maybe a photo album, or a diary would provide some clues, perhaps reveal a connection to my mother.

Most pet information was kept online now, but Maya had showed me a bookshelf full of leather binders that she still utilized. The word "personal" on one of them set off an alarm bell in my brain. Check it out, I told myself.

One afternoon while Maya was at a meeting with the

Humane Society, I entered her office and sat down in the padded office chair that reminded me of Mrs. Dimelroot's rolling chair at school. I was quite hopeful and excited. I had no idea what I might discover.

Each binder had a typed label on the spine. One said, "Nemo's History." I pulled the binder down and found many photos of the gentle Newfoundland swimming in a lake and one of him pulling children on a sled. Nemo once had a family he loved. How sad his owner didn't want him. Next, I found a notebook labeled "Pet History" with typed names of dogs, dates, brief descriptions and the names and addresses of new forever homes. So far, I had found nothing that helped me.

The "Personal" folder I had once noticed was nowhere to be found, so I opened the drawers of Maya's desk. Beyond boxes of cherry cough drops, Kleenex and dog toys were some paper tablets, way in the back. Under them, I discovered a packet of photos held together by a faded purple ribbon. High school dance photos, I decided. A pretty red-haired girl beamed from the pictures as various cute high school boys held the girl's hand or stood with an arm around her waist. Maya? She was so slim and no glasses or frizzed hair. In fact, her hair was long and straight. There were also photos of Maya at the shelter with her arms around various dogs like Halo and Mobley. In a few pictures, Mr. Will and Bjorn waved from the back ground.

I enjoyed snooping in Maya's office, but at the end of an hour, I had no new information—no clues to why Mom had chosen this animal shelter. Fortunately, I soon got over my disappointment. School was keeping me busy, and my detective plans got sidelined.

CHAPTER
NINETEEN

A few days later on a sunny Monday afternoon, Mrs. Dimelroot stood in front of the class and announced that Mr. McNulty was returning from Canada. She told us he was on a red eye flight from Toronto, would arrive home at two in the morning, catch a couple hours of sleep, and be at school by six for an early morning meeting.

Finally at 7:30, Mr. McNulty would return to our classroom. The whole class cheered. Mrs. Dimelroot shushed us and warned us Mr. McNulty would be tired, that we should be on our best behavior. She reminded us not to talk out of turn, fly paper airplanes, pass notes or be on our cell phones without permission.

Mrs. Dimelroot did not tell the class her early morning meeting was about me. I only knew because she had called Maya and requested that I come to school early to meet Mr. McNulty before the morning bell rang. Prior to my introduction, he was to be briefed about my progress. Maya wanted to attend too, but Mrs. Dimelroot explained this introductory meeting was only for certified members of the faculty.

On Tuesday I got up early. Maya fixed me breakfast and

rushed me out the door. The McNulty briefing was to be held in the library conference room. Our class often visited the library, so I knew the exact location. When I arrived at the library, I slipped in through the unlocked doors and walked up and down the shadowy stacks of books that loomed over me like castle walls.

When I reached the conference room, a welcoming beam of light greeted me through the half open door. Through the glass windows, I could see a group of teachers huddled around a formica table. They were crammed into student chairs, listening attentively to Mrs. Dimelroot. I glanced at the big red digital clock on the wall. It was only 6:30, and I was not supposed to arrive until 6:45. I turned away and wandered around the library, but I couldn't see much in the shadows, so I pulled up a chair outside the meeting room and sat down next to a wall of books. Mrs. Dimelroot was speaking in a loud voice. She was talking about me. I could hear every word.

"Borgia wrote this about herself," she said. "It's from the class autobiography assignment. She describes herself in the third person. Odd and strange. Read it aloud to the group, please, Mr. McNulty." Whoa, so the man sitting next to her was my new teacher Mr. McNulty. I stared at him. He was much younger than Mrs. Dimelroot. His hair was a bit messy, and he looked tired. He was frowning, but I thought he had a kind face.

"Call me John," Mr. McNulty said, leaning forward to take the paper.

"All right John." Mrs. Dimelroot folded her arms and waited.

Mr. McNulty cleared his throat and began to read aloud. "Borgia's hair seemed always to be blowing. Even in a silent, no-pin-dropping classroom, where students pressed their feet to the floor and folded their hands atop their desk, Borgia had an <u>aberrant</u> (vocab word list 7), tumbled <u>countenance</u> (vocab word list 9), that turned heads. Teachers placed a small check beside Borgia's name on the class list, a student to watch, to give an extra glance to during the day." Mr. McNulty set my paper down and looked around the table at the other teachers. "Borgia has an excellent vocabulary."

"The point is not her vocabulary, John. Borgia's ideas are not normal. Besides, those are words from lists I assigned to the class." Mrs. Dimelroot frowned and tapped her pen on the table. "Borgia struggles with reality. You will see that soon enough, but her paragraph gives you an idea of her unusual mental state."

"Anything else?" Mr. McNulty said, as if he hoped Mrs. Dimelroot was done.

"She has dark moods," Mrs. Dimelroot continued, looking round the table. That was true, I often missed my mom. I looked around the room at the other faces. The faculty looked groggy. The table was unsteady. It wobbled every few minutes. I decided the staff looked "disheveled"–another vocabulary word, messy much as the loose papers strewn over the round table were untidy. Their small student chairs sat too close to the ground; the teachers looked more like students than adults. The neatly pressed and pinned Mrs. Dimelroot presided over them with an alert relish, her padded office chair rising and falling according to its levers. She looked happy to be back in her counseling job out of the noisy classroom. Here, in charge of a sleepy faculty, she seemed truly in command.

"Is Borgia the girl with the straw-colored hair that looks like it's blowing?" Mr. McNulty asked. "I scrolled through the winter carnival pictures online."

" Yes, and now she has streaks of green," my PE teacher Mr. Bosker said. Then he leaned over and half whispered, "Like you, McNulty, green, rather callow, a new guy, not fully integrated into the profession."

"Not funny," Mr. McNulty said, and his face turned red. "You are about as dense as your barbells, Bosker. Not clever at all."

"Borgia seems morose a lot of the time," Mrs. Dimelroot added in a loud voice as if trying to squelch the angry side bar conversation between the two men. "She is obviously not on the same path as the other children."

Mr. McNulty took a gulp of coffee slurping loudly. On hearing this last comment from Mrs. Dimelroot, he slammed his mug down on the table. "Pardon me," he said, turning an even deeper shade of red. "I don't think we know what path most of these kids are on."

All eyes turned on him. There was a pregnant pause. Mr. McNulty looked overheated in his heavy sweater, not the best choice as the radiator cranking hot air kept the library very warm.

Mr. Minker the choir teacher interrupted, "You just got back, John. You haven't been here for any of this new kid's bizarre antics. Borgia needs special attention. Her crazy hairdos attract insects. When she is standing next to other students in choir, it makes it difficult for them to stay in key—all the flies buzzing about."

What! I sat upright and quit leaning on the library books. My hair only attracted bees once, not flies. That comment made me mad. Maybe on the winter carnival day, yes, but I remembered other days when there were flies. That was because Osa Langley, who stood next to me, often ate sardines from a small tin. Occasionally, he even threw a smelly fish at the girls in the row below him. On those days we all smelled fishy by the time choir class was over.

"Attention and staying in key are something entirely different than attaching obscure labels to a child," Mr. McNulty retorted, ignoring the part about my hair.

"Yeah, what if you find out she's living in a dog crate with the hounds? That shelter is a weird place. Giant wolf of a dog scaring people that walk by. I know, I live just down the road." Mr. Minker nodded and looked round the table. "Those wailing hounds are never in key." He smiled as if he had just cracked a funny joke.

"You aren't dealing with an everyday, hopscotch kid, John." This comment came from Clara Stark, the teacher in the room next to Mrs. Dimelroot. Maya told me she was glad I did not get Mrs. Stark for a teacher. She had a reputation for getting into conflicts with parents.

"What about that tale she was born in the Everglades and had gators for pets?" Mr. Bosker piped up.

"Who cares?" McNulty muttered under his breath. I saw Mrs. Dimelroot purse her lips smugly as if the scales were tipping in her favor.

"We have it on record that Borgia's birthplace was right here in Seattle, not the Everglades," she said, sifting through some papers on the table. "Her Aunt Maya filed papers with Erma, the head secretary. I admit I considered calling Child Protective Services when I realized she was not progressing socially or academically."

I knew it! My pulse raced. The words "Child Protective Services" set off an alarm in my brain.

I watched Mr. McNulty pull on his collar as if it felt scratchy. His right foot was tapping nervously under the table. "I'm trying to get a grip on this situation," he said. "True, unlike all of you, I only have a provisional teaching certificate and a one-year contract. I don't want to alienate the staff, but I don't agree with the conclusions you are reaching. Give me a chance with this kid, before you tell me what I need to do." As he spoke, he flipped off his shoe and accidentally sent his worn loafer flying into the leg of school counselor, Maxine Kinsman.

"Oh," she exclaimed as the flying shoe hit her shin. Reaching under the table, Mr. McNulty fished back his battered loafer. A new shade of crimson flamed on his face, and he grinned foolishly. Miss Kinsman looked distracted. I thought her eyes betrayed her, as if she too could not quite buy into the drama being created by Mrs. Dimelroot.

"My bad," Mr. McNulty said apologetically, "Sorry."

I felt sorry for Mr. McNulty. Mrs. Dimelroot seemed to be annoyed with him, just like she was with me. It was hard to tell what the others thought, but some obviously sided with Mrs. Dimelroot. All the teachers looked bleary eyed. It was so early in the morning. The day was barely underway.

Mr. McNulty began to maneuver a pink pearl eraser on the table. Set it up. Knock it over. "Maybe a one-year contract isn't such a bad deal," he said, thinking out loud. "Selling hotdogs in the fresh air from an open food truck has appeal, maybe street tacos." I looked at the curling countertops behind him, surfaces that hinted at black mold. For the first time I noticed how dingy the conference room was. Maybe he was right.

"Now, John," Mrs. Dimelroot said. "Calm down, we are not here to fire you." The others nodded.

"All right," he said. "Do you have any more records for me?"

"Yes, right here." Mrs. Dimelroot held up a neat file of papers held together by a paper clip. "Borgia's bright, no question. That type always is."

"May I look?" Mr. McNulty held out his hand. I noticed eyebrows raise around him. Did I detect a slight glint of admiration in Miss Kinsman's eyes? Apparently, no one else planned to challenge Mrs. Dimelroot's evaluation. I suddenly felt like I was sinking. I could feel my pulse racing. I leaned against the books again, and several of them fell on the floor with a thud. No one in the meeting seemed to notice.

"Information is missing because Borgia is not living with

her parents," Mrs. Dimelroot said, also handing him a slim manilla folder. "Borgia claims to have been homeschooled. She is behind academically and socially, no matter how you look at it. At times she acts much younger than her age."

Mrs. Dimelroot's last comment made me mad. I stood up and walked into the room.

"Borgia!" Mrs. Dimelroot said, obviously surprised. How long have you been out there?"

"Long enough to hear you say, I am behind, and you plan to call Child Protective Services." My voice was quavering, my hands shaking. "Not fair, I deserve a chance. This is my first time at a public school."

Mr. McNulty stood up. "Hi, Borgia. I'm John McNulty, your new teacher. Happy to meet you. I agree. You deserve a chance."

Everyone around the table looked sheepish. Miss Kinsman clapped. Then they all clapped, that is everyone except Mrs. Dimelroot, who pursed her lips and wrinkled her forehead.

"Bravo, Kiddo," Mr. Bosker, my PE teacher, was saying. Miss Kinsman smiled at me. Only Mrs. Dimelroot looked as if the meeting had not gone as expected.

TWENTY

O n the same day that I sat in the library waiting to meet Mr. McNulty for the first time, I was carrying a black velvet purse, another treasure Maya discovered for me at Value Village. Since the Winter Carnival, Maya had also taken me to the fabric store. Not my favorite place. I found sewing and patterns boring, but I consented to help Maya pick out material so she could sew me a new spring dress.

She made me three outfits, and I was wearing one of the dresses today, sleeveless covered with green alligators. In keeping with the reptile theme, a long green tail protruded from my purse, a plastic iguana I purchased for a quarter at Goodwill, quite used, so the ratty tail looked like it might crack off at any moment.

Mrs. Dimelroot had been so critical of me that morning, I felt both rebellious and wounded. I also felt tough and hardened like a walnut. Nobody was going to crack me open. When I entered the Arrowridge cafeteria at lunchtime, I was ready to battle the world.

"Is that a crocodile you got in that ugly bag?" Craig Bunger looked up from smashing milk cartons with his foot. He laughed every time a carton popped, making some of the kids jump–even drop their sandwiches. Now he paused and surveyed me from head to toe.

His friend Randall yelled, "Look at the crocs on her dress. Don't you know, Borgia was raised by crocs down in swampy Florida. See that green tail coming out of her purse. Probably has a croc in there right now."

"Silly," I said. "Crocodiles don't come from Florida. I was raised by alligators." I leaned over and glared straight into Randall's freckled face. Next to him, Langston Bulip sputtered into his straw, spewing chocolate milk bubbles from his nose.

"Major gross out," one of the girls sniffed from across the table.

Osa Langley, another member of the gang, followed close on my heels, yelling, "Maybe we can find a gator to visit you in your cage at the dog shelter."

"Maybe I will ride an alligator to school and make you examine its teeth," I snapped back, my voice stiff as a fall breeze. I was not about to let Osa make me cry, even if he did ignite my temper. My green hair flew behind me as I strode away in blue and green sneakers. The green streaks matched my gator stories.

I had learned first-hand how to be dramatic. Mom insisted drama was an important part of life. Maya was rather dramatic herself. Being flamboyant helped insulate me from these creepy kids. Mei Ling told me, there are always mean kids in a school, no matter what the adults do to try and stop them.

Only the tough kids challenged me, said I didn't know what I was talking about. I lashed back at them, and gradually their bravado faded. As the weeks wore on, some of the worst bullies began to treat me with a degree of respect not usually afforded an arty kid in a STEM-oriented world. Osa dug his hands into his pockets and kicked at a stray sandwich wrapper on the floor.

"Borgia's trouble," I heard him mutter to one of his disheveled friends.

Mei Ling said the worst Arrowridge bullies had been together since preschool. No one seemed to be able to monitor what this gang of ruffians did before or after school. They knew how to evade discipline by pretending to be good as gold when questioned and to create sound alibis for each other. The current focus on antibullying made it more difficult to heckle someone without getting in trouble, but their group was famous for it. I liked to believe I had removed myself from their victim list with my staunch disdain for their insults and explosive retorts. I was feared and respected, rather than viewed as someone to squash.

Mei Ling, now my closest friend, whispered in my ear, "You are the queen in a chess game, playing against a row of scrappy pawns. The weak pieces try to annoy the queen, but you just shout, 'off with your heads,' and the bullies scatter, tumble off the board. Game over!" I smiled. Mei Ling was on my side. It certainly helped to have a friend.

Being left alone by the bad boys of the school, made me feel better about myself. I still annoyed Mrs. Dimelroot, now my school counselor, after Mr. McNulty returned. She continued to insist my life had been influenced by too much drama. Mom was the queen of show boating. She loved to draw attention to herself, like wrapping up in Christmas lights. I thought being dramatic was an asset, but after a few intense weeks being dramatic at school, I got tired of showing off. It felt better to blend in rather than try to stand out.

Mei Ling walked alongside me while we discussed our problems. Talking to her helped anchor me. She said I was the most interesting girl in the school and way cooler than popular girls like Kimberly, who had started an exclusive girls' club called Crisscross. On Thursdays her friends wore plaid skirts with big safety pins on the side. Each week they added a new glass bead or silver charm to the pin. It looked really cool. The Crisscross girls all had the same mint green water bottles filled with kombucha, and they ate dainty cups of yogurt with flavors like kiwi and rose blossom. Sometimes I wished I was in their exclusive club.

Thank heavens, I had Mei Ling's friendship. When she smiled at me, it gave me confidence. She sat with me every day at lunch and complained about the 1000-page workbook as much as I did. She was an excellent student, the top math student in the whole school. She said she would help me with math and teach me how to show my work. Jim, the artist who sat next to me, handed me several sketches of alligators. Maya thought they were so realistic, she displayed his drawings on the refrigerator.

When Mr. McNulty first stood up in the classroom, he looked rumpled and tired, but he smiled, and all the kids cheered, happy to have him back. He even leaned down over my desk and told me I could call him McNut like all the other kids did. I did not have to use the "Mr." Then he called me back to his desk and talked to me individually. He typed some notes and checked what I would like to be called. He asked me to show him my plastic iguana and laughed when I told him about my dog Eightball. I liked him. With McNut back in the classroom, the day did not seem to drag. Maya even told me I seemed happy. Plus, I was growing taller. Hurrah. That was a start. I hated the idea that I acted younger than my age, like some giant baby.

TWENTY-ONE

The weeks flew by, and I was still at the shelter. One morning, Maya announced, "I am going to build a chicken coop."

"How do you do that?" I asked.

"First step, pay a visit to Mr. Will. See if he can help me. Want to come along?"

It was Saturday. I had no plans, so after breakfast, I followed Maya down the main road until we reached the black and yellow road sign. From there we headed up hill until we reached a huge turn-around driveway and a sprawling modern building with a covered entry that looked like a fancy hotel. Big pots of feathery plants waved in the breeze. Maya said the plants were pampas grass. A sign over the portico said, "Pampered Pets Purebred Spa and Boarding." We passed by the main office with gleaming windows and walked under heavy cedar beams and giant wood carvings of dogs, then continued up the driveway and came upon row after row of spotless kennels.

"Wanted you to see my competition," Maya said, pointing out the fancy cages with elaborate dog beds. "Actually, it's not my competition at all. Only purebred dogs are allowed here. My dogs are mostly mixed breed or purebred with no papers. Everything at the spa is state of the art. There are dog showers, indoor walking tracks, play rooms, grooming and shampoo stalls, even a canine swimming pool." Maya sounded envious. "A veterinarian is always on site, and many of the older dogs get Chinese acupuncture and Vitamin B12 shots to help them when their legs start to go." I had to admit the Purebred Spa was in stark contrast to Maya's bare bones animal shelter, held loosely together by volunteers and Maya's kind heart.

The Pampered Pets Purebred Dog Spa and Boarding was surrounded by well-groomed walking trails and dotted by stainless steel bowls of water. The paths were marked by signs with names like Poodle Avenue and Golden Doodle Row. Even I admired the place, but Maya seemed eager to leave and made a sharp turn, stepping onto a dirt trail that headed into the deep woods.

I liked the forest, but I soon got tired of brush and brambles hitting me in the face and scratching my arms. "Does Mr. Will really live out here somewhere?" I groused to Maya, just as we emerged into a clearing with a wide mossy lawn. In the middle of the lawn sprawled a two-story home that looked like it had been built of Lincoln logs. A river rock chimney ran up the end of the house. Maya clumped up the steps of the wrap-around porch and passed by three big rocking chairs. I followed and stood next to her as she clapped the dolphin knocker on the front door.

"Mr. Will's and Danielle's place," she said, sweeping her hand past a distant barn and a rolling pasture with a white fence. "A perfect little farm." I hadn't met Mr. Will's wife yet, but she answered the door and gave Maya a big hug. She smiled at me and shook my hand as Maya introduced me. Danielle said she and Maya were old friends from high school.

"Thanks for coming," she said to Maya. "I have meetings all

day so a project at the shelter is just right to keep Mr. Will busy." She laughed. I wanted to ask her why everyone called him Mr. Will. Later Maya told me it was a southern thing and he was from the South.

While Maya and Danielle were chatting, Mr. Will appeared behind them rubbing his hands together. He was already talking and smiling at the same time. Behind him, two large curly haired dogs wagged their tails.

"Gotta run," Danielle said. "Conference call is about to begin. Great to meet you, Borgia. Visit us anytime." She smiled, then turned to Maya. " One chicken coop coming right up, and here is the man who can help you."

"Come in, come in," Mr. Will said, stepping forward. "By golly, was just thinking about that coop you mentioned, Maya. Drew up some plans. Nice to see you, Borgia. Remy is home today, down working on his drones in the basement."

I must have looked confused, because Maya explained, "Remy is Mr. Will and Danielle's son." Did I already know this? I guess I forgot.

We walked past a dining room table with a bowl full of rocks as a centerpiece. On the wall a cuckoo clock was chiming. A little robotic bird popped out a tiny door and chirped the hour. Mr. Will led us through the kitchen and down steep wooden stairs. "Hold onto the railing," he said. "These stairs are like going down a slide."

The basement appeared to be a giant workroom. At the far end, a young boy sat at a table, bent over a miniature airplane.

"Remy, this is Borgia," Mr. Will kept talking, but I wasn't really listening. I stared at the dark-haired boy who stood up and politely extended his hand.

"Hi," Remy said and fell silent while his dad continued to talk. "Borgia is the girl who moved in with Maya, remember. I was hoping—"

Just then Maya, who had stayed upstairs because of her bad knees, called down, "Phil, you coming back up?"

"Good golly, gotta go," Mr. Will said, smiling. "Borgia, want to stay down here and keep Remy company?" I shrugged.

"Phillll," Maya called again.

Mr. Will wrung his hands. "Gotta go."

All the way up the stairs, Mr. Will kept talking, something about Remy and drones. Only when the door at the top of the stairs closed, did a stony silence settle over the cavernous basement. For some reason, I didn't mind. Remy returned to twisting a coil of blue wire with a pair of needle-nosed pliers. Without looking up or taking his eyes off his work, he said, "I like your green hair, same color as my siphon drone." He pointed his pliers at a green contraption next to him. No one had ever compared my hair to a drone before.

"Your dad likes dogs," I said, not sure what else to say.

"No kidding," Remy, said. "Are you a dog nut too?"

I had to think about that, considering all the complaining I had done recently. "I guess so. I like dogs, but sometimes they drive me crazy." Remy looked at me directly for the first time. He had hazel eyes with lines around them.

"I get it," he said. "Sometimes Dad talks so much about shelter dogs, I get jealous. I wish he had more interest in the things I'm working on."

"Your planes are cool. Did you design them yourself?"

"Kinda. Most of them are drone kits, but I mix and match." I think I get my engineering genes from my mom. She works for Google. I'm not an animal lover like Dad."

"I just met your mom for the first time too." I eased down on a folding chair next to him.

"Mom works in the city. She doesn't volunteer at the kennel. Truth is, she is allergic to dog hair. That's why we have Labradoodles. They don't shed. She and Maya both attended

Roosevelt High School. They get together here at our house, not so much dog hair."

"Oh," I said. "I never see you at school either."

"I go to a private school in Seattle." Remy set his pliers down and started working on a propeller. "Mom drops me off on her way to work. In four years, I can drive myself."

"So, you are twelve," I said, doing the math.

"Yeah, how about you?"

My heart skipped a beat. Then I surprised myself with a direct and truthful answer, "I don't know. My mom never kept records." I felt somewhat humiliated by this information.

"Seriously," Remy said, once again looking at me directly with his intense eyes. "That is so cool. You don't know your age? That's like some character in a novel or a movie." He set the propellers down on the work bench and turned to face me.

I stared at my hands. "I guess, but most people seem creeped out by it. Adults can't deal with it at all."

"Surprise, surprise," Remy said, smiling. "I think I am older than you. I'm taller, anyway. He stood up and I stood next to him. He must have been two inches taller than me. "Wait, how will you know when you are old enough to drive?" Driving was obviously very important to Remy.

"I don't want to drive," I wrinkled my nose.

Remy raised his eyebrows, then grinned. "I guess if you don't know your age, you can't get a driver's license anyway. How will you get around then? Take a Lyft?"

"Ride a horse," I said, without thinking. I had only been on the pony rides at the Zoo, but I was crazy about horses.

"Really!" Remy said. "Maybe you would like to ride our horse. Bello is an ex-racehorse, rescued from a neighbor who couldn't take care of him anymore. He needs exercise. Someone has to ride him. Right now, it's me."

"You own a horse?"

"Yeah. We got him because we have a big empty pasture and an old barn. Dad expects me to take care of him, but I am not a horse fan."

"Your own horse?" I said, my eyes widening.

"Kinda. He's more like my main chore. Want to see him?"

"Are you kidding?" I totally wanted to see him.

CHAPTER
TWENTY-TWO

Before I knew it, I was following Remy up the steep stairs and out across his wide lawn toward the pasture. A warm breeze played over my face. I felt happy.

"Are you into music like your dad?" I asked, when we reached the white fence. Remy swung open an aluminum gate and led me past an old barn with a sagging roof weighted down with green moss.

"Nope, I like music, but my dad is a music encyclopedia."

"So I noticed."

"There's Bello." Remy pointed to a brown horse swishing his tail under a maple tree. He handed me an orange carrot still attached to a tassel of green leaves. "Feed Bello a carrot, he's your friend forever. Bello, Carrot!" The horse raised his head, pricked up his ears and walked slowly toward us in a very relaxed manner.

"He's so tall," I said. "So much larger than the ponies at the Zoo. I bet he can run like the wind."

"Yep, he jumps, too. See how high the fence is? We had to add an extra rung. When Bello first arrived, he would sail over this fence and trot all over the neighborhood, tearing up people's lawns. Fortunately, he trotted home at night to get the oats we fed him. We raised the fence higher, but to be fair to him, we put up a couple low jumps here in the pasture. Bello leaps over them for fun."

"Cool," I said. "I wish I knew how to ride." I suddenly felt foolish and a bit of a fraud, earlier claiming I knew how to ride from being led around on a pony at the Zoo.

"It's a cinch," Remy said. "Easy peasy." The giant horse reached out his long neck and eagerly took the carrot from Remy's outstretched palm, revealing huge, stained teeth. "Hold your hand flat like this," Remy said, handing me a carrot. "Heh, heh, Bello loves to eat, don't you, big Fellow? His ribs showed before we rescued him. His hooves were cracked, and he was covered with yellow horsefly eggs. Poor guy."

"He certainly looks fit now. He smells good, too." I patted his sturdy neck.

"Yeah, I guess if you like the scent of horses." Remy held a complicated bridle up to Bello's head and slipped a metal bit into his mouth. Next, he gently pulled the dark mane hair out from under the leather strap and fanned it across his forehead. "Got to look good, right Bello?"

I smiled at Remy talking gently to the horse. His positive voice and friendly manner reminded me of his dad. I reached up and patted the horse again, amazed by how much dust rose from his coat.

"Kind of a dirty guy," Remy said. "You don't mind being dusty, huh big boy?"

"What color is he?" I asked. I had studied horses in home school, but I could not identify this color.

"Dad says he's a bay. See his dark legs? In horse language they call them stockings." Remy hooked a thick rope to the metal ring on Bello's bridle and had me hold it while he threw a red and yellow blanket over his back, then placed a leather saddle on top of that. Once the saddle cinch was fastened tightly under his belly, he placed his foot in the stirrup and swung up onto the horse. It was fascinating.

Pulling the reins, Remy turned Bello out into the pasture moving at a brisk trot. His whole body bounced like crazy. I laughed. Remy looked like he would tumble off at any moment. On his next round past, he leaned over where I perched on the edge of the fence and pulled me on behind him. Now I bumped along with him too, trying not to slide off.

"Hold on to me," Remy said. He pulled on the reins, and the horse slowed to a more even and gentle walk. After a few minutes, we stopped under the big maple tree.

"Your turn to be in front," Remy said, tying the reins together in a knot.

"I can't possibly," I sputtered, but Remy insisted.

"No excuses. You can do it." He slipped out of the saddle and slid to the ground. "Scoot forward. Hey, you look great up there. Just give Bello a nudge with your feet. Here, I'll place your feet properly in the stirrups."

Sitting high in that saddle for the first time, my hands on the reins, a brand-new world opened. I patted the horse's neck as we moved off across the pasture at a slow walk. Bello swished his tail. His ears kept going back and forth like he was listening to me. Exhilarated, I felt free. The sound of his hooves and the cadence of his walk created a music all its own. I felt so proud. I could not believe I was riding a horse all by myself.

Later, back on the fence, I watched while Remy took Bello over a couple of jumps. One jump was made of orange plastic webbing, another fashioned out of old wooden sawhorses. Bello sailed over each one, arching his powerful neck and folding his huge legs gracefully. "Magnificent, huh?" yelled Remy. I nodded, mesmerized. This horse loved to jump.

"I will teach you how to jump too, Borgia, but we'll save it for another day." Remy lifted the saddle off Bello's back and led him around the pasture to cool off. "See how damp he is. Horses sweat just like people. You never want to put a lathered horse away wet. They can get really sick. Dad, of course, has made me read all about how to care for Bello, so I am learning more than I ever wanted to know about horses."

I smiled. I could imagine Mr. Will going on and on about horse care.

"I am excited you want to ride," Remy said, as he latched the metal gate, and we headed back to the basement. I could not believe my luck. I would be ready to ride again as soon as Remy had the time.

When Maya reappeared at the top of the stairs, ready to walk me home, she had no idea, how in one afternoon, my life had changed. I felt somewhat reluctant to leave Mr. Will's home, but I waved good bye and wondered when I would see Remy again. Maya asked if I had a good time. She had no idea.

CHAPTER

TWENTY-THREE

I walked over to Remy's house almost every weekend and sometimes after school. He arrived home much later than I did. "I think you come to see Bello, not me," Remy said, laughing. "I am good with that."

I liked Remy, but the chance to groom and ride a horse was a stardust wish come true that eclipsed everything else. Horse care never felt like work. Every detail was fascinating. Remy showed me how to slip the bridle over Bello's ears, then hoist the heavy saddle on to his back and cinch it tight. He was eager to teach me, because he wanted a break. I savored the sweet smell of the leather mixed with warm horse flesh.

I grew so comfortable spending time with Remy, that I was shocked one afternoon to find another kid sitting next to him in the basement. Both were bent intently over the workbench. I thought about hurrying back up the stairs, but Remy saw me first.

"Lump, meet Borgia." Remy flipped around and pointed at me with a pair of pliers, while he nodded to the older kid.

"My real name is Lawrence," the heavyset boy said, without looking up, "but I prefer to be called Lump."

"Lump is my cousin," Remy added. "He likes robotics as much as I do."

"More than you do," Lump said, turning over a small motor. "I would say at least 20% more than you, Remy."

"Lump is sixteen. He can drive," Remy said, ignoring his response. "Got his license three months ago. He plans to convert Dad's old Fiat into a driverless car."

"Yep," Lump agreed, as he pulled on a pair of goggles. Lump certainly didn't have a lot to say. Soon, sparks were flying all around him. He looked like a mad scientist. Remy and I left Lump in the basement bent over his fiery motor and walked side by side out to the barn. A warm breeze played on my face and sunlight splattered the ground.

"Jumping class today," Remy said. I took a deep breath. Bello loved to jump, but I was not sure I did. I brushed my hair out of my eyes and tried to look enthusiastic.

While I sat on the fence, watching Remy and Bello soar over makeshift jumps, I panicked. This huge animal with its sharp hooves folded in the air was terrifying. "Too scary!" I yelled at Remy as he cantered past. Smack in the middle of a jump, I was certain I would tumble off on the hard, hard ground.

"That's fine," Remy said agreeably, pulling up on the reins. "I think you're ready, but you get to decide. Maybe next weekend." He helped me up into the stirrup, and as I eased into the saddle, he waved good bye and headed back to the basement. I was confident enough to ride alone. I patted Bello's neck and took the reins. At this point I was happy to walk, trot and once in a while, canter around the pasture. That was it.

Two weekends later, I announced, "I'm ready to learn how to jump." Remy gave me a thumbs up. It was easier than I thought. Bello did all the work, and I could tell he loved it. We agreed I would never take Bello over a jump unless Remy or Mr. Will was there.

Eventually, I got permission to ride Bello along the road. My usual route was to follow the white fence down a dirt path to the yellow road sign , then up hill to the fancy dog spa. Here, I always paused and admired the formal entryway. Trainers were usually out walking the handsome purebred dogs. All wore dark green polo shirts with a Labrador retriever embroidered on the right pocket. Maya said the spa workers were paid employees, not like Maya's shelter, where Mr. Will and others volunteered their time.

CHAPTER

TWENTY-FOUR

N ow that I rode horseback regularly, time seemed to fly. My life was also brimful with school, friends, and of course, dogs. I still missed Mom, but I did not have a moment to spare and feel sorry for myself. Much of my loneliness and anger had evaporated too. The world around me was changing. One afternoon Lump even offered to give Remy and me a ride in the little sea-green Fiat. I said I would rather watch.

"Can you believe Lump got this wreck going?" Mr. Will stood admiring the little car, his voice full of pride. He threw both hands in the air as if he was going to embrace the vehicle when Lump roared by, spinning doughnut circles on the gravel drive. Looked like showing off to me.

"Lump and Remy together can manage just about any car, drone or plane, but I'm glad someone around here is focused on dogs and horses." After saying this, Mr. Will tilted his head at me knowingly, as if he considered my focus quite a miracle. "Oh, I meant to tell you, I ordered a special pair of rubber shoes to protect Bello's hooves when you walk him on asphalt roads."

"Great," I said, even though I had no idea what Mr. Will

was talking about. From then on Bello wore rubber shoes whenever I rode on paved streets, I guess to protect his tender hooves.

While Mr. Will was talking about the rubber shoes, I stole a glance at the calendar on my cell phone and realized I had been attending public school for over two months. Now that McNut, OK, Mr. McNulty was back, I actually looked forward to class. Sometimes I even got excited over assignments. Plus, I no longer spent much energy trying to be dramatic. It was OK just to be myself.

Mei Ling continued to teach me how to be a good friend. We slipped secret notes to each other in class and made faces signaling our emotions. Mei Ling could wiggle her nose better than anyone else and cross her eyes to register displeasure. She often made me laugh. Sometimes McNut frowned at me when Mei Ling was actually the cause of my giggles.

The weather was changing too. The snow had melted long ago, and bright purple and yellow crocuses were nosing up out of the ground. Maya and I still wore heavy jackets in the morning when we walked the dogs, but a hint of spring always wafted in the air. The sunshine breaking through clouds seemed a little brighter each day. Most of the time, I no longer zipped up my coat.

Saturdays, I generally puttered around the shelter, helping Maya before heading over to check on Remy and Bello. One particular Saturday, after hosing down kennels, rinsing out water bowls and petting as many dogs as possible, I stood on the bottom rung of the pasture gate, watching the pygmy goats pose on top of the woodpile.

Halo the Great Pyrenees lay nearby in the grass keeping an eye on his flock. The huge dog had quickly accepted me as part of Maya's pack and no longer barked when I got close. I suspect he kept an eye on me, too. I was just about to return to the kennels and head over to Remy's, when I heard a car idling outside the chain link fence.

A forever home for one of the dogs was my first thought. A strange car often meant a new family. Watching an animal leave with strangers was both happy and sad. We lost a friend. Maya never seemed to mind, but I struggled to say good-bye. The little dogs found homes a lot easier than the big dogs, even though the big dogs were the most gentle and loyal.

As I shaded my eyes to get a better view, a slim figure stepped out of the car. A tall woman ran a hand through her short hair, and my heart stopped. I jumped down from the fence and ran. It was my mother.

"Mom," I screamed. She reached out and embraced me. I could not believe it. A huge weight lifted from my heart. Through Mom's arms, I could see Maya in her black gum boots, standing in a kennel doorway watching us.

"Maya, my mom's here!" Maya, usually so friendly, continued to stand like a statue, an especially stern expression on her face. Then Mom surprised me. She unwrapped my arms, took my hand and walked forward.

"Hello Maya," she said. "Thank you for taking care of Borgia. I knew she would be safe with you."

"Hey," I said, puzzled. "You know each other?"

"Maya is my sister," Mom said. "She's your aunt." Maya didn't move a muscle.

"What?" I said incredulously. "What? Why didn't anybody tell me?" Maya turned and walked back into the kennel.

"Maya and I don't speak to each other," Mom said, looking down at me. "Boy, it reeks of dogs here. Whew," she waved her hand in the air. "How can you stand it, Borgia?"

Mom and Maya were sisters? My mind was reeling. I turned back to Mom.

"Where have you been? I've been so worried."

"I've been rattled," Mom said, using one of her favorite phrases that always made me think of earthquakes and snake bites, not people.

"Ever since the houseboat blew up, my life has been out of control. Crazy!"

This sounded so like Mom, always focusing on how upset she was. "Del and I had to anchor the Paris trip or lose it. Marley insisted we fly to Toronto. Had to meet the Canadian bands that will perform with us. Fortunately, the Paris trip is now a reality."

"That's great, Mom, but why did the police arrest you? Was it because of me?"

"Complicated, but yeah, when you put that glow necklace on, it was like shining a spotlight on your underage self. A security guard reported a child on stage. He said you were breaking the law, performing with our band. No joke. Took a while to sort out all the accusations— kid on stage, sinking houseboat, and missing jewelry. Del and I had the book thrown at us. Not fair. We're not criminals. The fireworks fiasco was an accident. The police used the handcuffs to make a point, terrifying. Still haunts me."

I could hardly bear to listen. "Mom," I said, my voice wrenching with emotion. "You left me. You said you would never leave me."

"I'm here now." A sharp edge grated in Mom's voice. "I drove all the way out to this zoo to get you." Just then Eightball appeared, running at high speed straight for us. Mom screamed.

"Don't worry, Mom. It's only Eightball. He's my dog"

"You have a dog?" Mom's voice cracked, and she wrinkled her nose.

"Yeah, and I ride horseback. I go to school." Wow, I was telling Mom everything in one fell swoop.

Mom looked down at me, frowning. Giant, panting Eight-ball was drooling slime all over my leg. He lifted a muddy paw and tried to get Mom's attention, but she backed away just in time.

"You surprise me, Borgia. I don't know what to say. I expected you to be suffering here. Far from it, obviously." She smoothed her coat and pulled up her purse strap that always slid off her narrow shoulders.

Wow, that was true. "Mom," I said, without missing a beat. "I made some friends, kids my own age. School is hard, but I like my teacher. If you need a place to stay, I think Maya would welcome you."

Mom's face dropped. She looked stunned like I had slapped her. As we stood there, both looking shocked, Maya walked towards us from the kennels, holding her rubber gloves in one hand. Now she looked more like the reasonable Maya I knew.

"Borgia is right," she said. "I welcome you, Rose. Stay with me; we can start over."

Mom set her jaw. "I go by Celia, not Rose. I could never live with all these animals. I'm allergic to dogs." As if on cue, she sneezed. "Borgia, run to the car and get the box of Kleenex in the glove compartment." I ran. I always did what Mom said.

CHAPTER
TWENTY-FIVE

Mom refused to spend even one night at the shelter. At the moment, she and Del were camping at Lionel's apartment. Sleeping on an uncomfortable sofa had hurt her back. She said I could stay there, too. I shivered at the thought. I did not want to sleep in Lionel's creepy apartment with all the globby, orange lava lamps and the collection of rusty sculptures he had welded together out of metal gears found at a wrecking yard.

"I came to pick you up, Borgia, but Lionel is not happy about adding one more person to his cramped apartment. You can imagine. I thought maybe we could make a bed for you in the Coffin until I can get my own place."

"I'd have to sleep in the car? Outside?"

"It's not so bad. I've done it before. The windows are already blacked out, and we park it right next to the ground floor window of Lionel's bedroom. I know he would leave the window open, so we could keep an eye on you, hear you if you screamed." Mom gave me a wry smile. The idea sounded more and more terrible.

"Borgia can stay with me until you find a place," Maya

said, seeing the distress on my face. "In fact, she can stay here as long as she likes." I sighed with relief. I did not want to sleep in a car alone at night, especially right outside Lionel's window. Maya's generous offer had the opposite effect on Mom. She looked like she was going to punch her in the stomach. Instead, she lifted her head and stared out at the deep forest like she was contemplating an escape from her sister.

"I'd like to stay here a while longer," I said, surprised by how good those words sounded.

Mom glanced down at me as if she could not believe her ears. After thinking for a bit, she spoke. "Staying on at the shelter for a while would solve the problem of what to do with you while I'm in France. Del and I leave for Paris with the band in a few weeks and tour for two months. When we get back, I should have enough money to rent my own place in Seattle. Then you can join me, Borgia."

"Look for another houseboat," I said wistfully. As I spoke, it dawned on me Eightball would have to live with us, too. Mom would have to deal with her allergies.

"Borgia can finish up the school year here," Maya added. Mom did not respond to that comment. Instead, she glanced at her watch, said she needed to get back.

Then she looked at me. "Do you mind staying with Maya while I travel?"

"I want to stay!" I said enthusiastically. Finally Mom and Maya agreed on something. As I watched Mom drive away, I tried hard not to be upset. Her old phone was now in my name. Her new one had a case with a red and gold zigzag pattern.

I turned to Maya, Aunt Maya. The word "Aunt" took on new meaning, now that the truth was out in the open. Maya and I were related, members of the same family. I had been turning the idea over ever since Greet knocked her photos onto the bedroom floor. I recognized something familiar in those two sisters, Maya and Rose.

"Will you tell me why you and Mom don't speak to each other?"

"Eventually," Maya said. Then she added, "Yes, yes, of course I will. Maybe I can figure it out, too."

"And," I said, feeling more than a little cross, "Why didn't you tell me you were my aunt? When did you figure out I was your niece?"

Maya looked sheepish. It turned out she had a hunch on the dog trail, clear back when she learned Mom's name was Celia. When I handed her Mom's purple phone, and she saw photos of her band Tides Out, she recognized her sister. "You deserve to know the truth, Borgia. I'll do my best. The subject is painful, not knowing I had a niece until you arrived at the shelter."

It became clear Maya was not going to talk about Mom unless I brought it up. After dinner, I approached Maya holding the framed photo Greet had knocked on the floor. The glass was still cracked. I was wearing the golden spur pin Mom had given me, like the one I had noticed in the photo. I pointed to the slim teenager staring out from the camera beside a little girl with pigtails, sitting on a tricycle. "You and Mom?" Maya nodded. She did not look at the photo but stared off into space as though trying to remember.

"Very sad, so stupid. Your mother is ten years younger. You may remember me telling you, my mom and dad divorced. Our mother remarried Albert Smith, my stepdad and your mother's father.

"I didn't get along with my stepfather. He tried so hard to control me—demanded I wear dresses to school. He expected my hair to be short, what he called a fashionable length. He hated my long hair, the casual bandanas and beads I often wore. Bellbottom pants were a big no-no in his book.

"Albert always wore a suit and tie. He was a businessman while I was a wild free spirit. I did not fit his mold. When I brought home a boy who sewed the American flag into his jeans, Albert forbade me to date him. I stormed off, moved in with my best friend. After I turned eighteen, there was nothing anyone could do to stop me. I refused to move to Florida when Albert was transferred. Naturally, I wanted to finish my senior year at Roosevelt High School and stay with my friends.

"Rose was only eight when they moved to Florida. She grew up without me. Somehow, I managed to get a scholarship to the University of Washington. Not long after, Mom died of lung cancer. I didn't see Rose for a long time. We wrote letters. That was it. I sent her my golden spur pin when I learned she was in high school. So happy she gave it to you. When I saw you had that pin, I began to wonder even more about your identity."

I touched the golden spur pin, even more special now. "So why don't you speak to each other?"

Maya sighed, "Rose moved back to Seattle after she graduated from high school. I was working as a social worker and had purchased a small house. I invited her to stay with me. I thought she should go to college, but she had no interest in higher education. When my stepdad passed away, he left everything to her, all his money and all of Mom's things.

"Rose and I began to argue over the most ridiculous objects–a glass bowl, an old quilt, even a pillow. She owned all of it legally, but I thought I deserved some of the family heirlooms, some of the money too. Rose accused me of trying to control her. She said I was bossy and put too much emphasis on a college degree.

"One day a small event broke the back of our relationship. I snapped her picture with a new camera. Rose had been adamant she did not want her picture taken. When I displayed the photo on social media, she exploded. 'That's it, Maya. You will never have power over me, ever again.'" She moved out. I tried to find her, but she changed her name, dyed her hair. I heard she had moved back to Florida.

"A year later, my birth father, passed away and left me a small inheritance—enough cash to purchase this animal shelter. That's when Rose contacted me and asked for some of my money. She had been scammed out of her inheritance and fallen on hard times. I said absolutely not, remembering how she treated me when I needed help. From then on, neither of us spoke to each other. It was so stupid. I lost contact with my only sister.

"Remember Christmas morning when all the dogs got loose on the trail? You said something that made me realize there was a real possibility your mom was my sister and you were my niece. What a surprise! The best Christmas gift I ever received."

I beamed. "Do you think Mom became Celia Harringa to avoid you?"

Maya shrugged her shoulders and blinked as if she might cry. "Maybe."

I ran and hugged her. "I won't ever abandon you, Maya."

"Sad, isn't it?" Maya sniffed. "But you found me, Borgia, and now we both have a new life. Rose even spoke to me again."

I smiled. Maya was family. I was going back to school. "You better learn to call her Celia. She doesn't like being called Rose."

CHAPTER

TWENTY-SIX

N ow I looked forward to school every day. Unlike Mrs. Dimelroot, Mr. McNulty made me feel smart. One of the first things McNut did when he took charge of our class was to get rid of the thousand-page workbooks that smelled like the disinfectant in gas station bathrooms. Exuberantly, our class stacked the heavy *Spring into the Future* workbooks in the back of the room and built a huge tower. We celebrated never having to turn another flimsy page, not to mention, no more tedious hours filling in blank lines and empty squares. So boring, could put anybody to sleep.

Only Kimberly was upset by the idea of discarding the workbooks. Way ahead of the class, she had already completed page 176, while I was still on page 23. Looking at Kimberly's stricken face as she watched the rest of us toss our workbooks onto the pile, Mr. McNulty said, "Kimberly, I admire your work ethic. You can keep your copy of *Spring into the Future*. Take it home. When you finish all 1000 pages, I will give you a reward."

McNut had lined up miscellaneous prizes and rewards on the window sill, doling them out when kids met or exceeded expectations. There was a silver pen, a penguin pennant, various sparkly markers and post it notes. For a long time, Kimberly had been hankering for the ceramic bear wearing a flower hat, that Mrs. Dimelroot donated to the class when she left. Kimberly hoped it might soon belong to her.

Unlike Kimberly, I was thrilled to part with my thousand pages and see my workbook wedged securely in the middle of the paper tower. I colored the spine purple and all the outside edges pink, adding a few blue polka dots like on my favorite swimming suit. Now I always knew which workbook was mine.

Just like my mom, McNut loved rock music. While we worked, building our class room tower, he played songs from Pink Floyd, music Mom and Del loved, too. I felt right at home singing about the brick in the wall with the rest of the class. McNut said he did not want to be remembered as the teacher who tortured his students by forcing them to fill a thousand pages that felt more like a million. My heart warmed when he said that. Mc Nut understood us. At least he understood me.

With the torturous workbook no longer clogging my mind, the drab lessons in futility evaporated. "Futility" was a vocabulary word I had just mastered. The first Monday of every month, each student chose one word from our personal reading to write on the whiteboard. We all crowded together, writing in cursive with the class set of rainbow markers. McNut chose ten student words and added five of his own. That was our vocabulary list.

Most amazing, once the workbooks were stacked in the back of the room, I no longer felt behind. Instead of spending hours trying to keep my mind focused on boring paragraphs, our class read entire chapter books. We also read complete poems, not just bits and pieces called excerpts. I liked reading entire books. Maybe there was nothing wrong with me after all. Mei Ling was so helpful at explaining math, I actually began to solve complex problems on my own. I liked PE. I loved chorus especially since no sardine eating was allowed, and the fly problem disappeared.

"Mr. McNulty," I said, one day after school, approaching him where he sat at his desk, sorting through a set of papers.

"What is it, Borgia?" He looked up at me with friendly concern, a day's growth of whiskers and dark circles under his eyes. Poor guy, he often looked tired. I guess teaching our class was hard work.

I swallowed. "Do you ever consider calling Child Protective Services? I know the school counselor thinks I need special attention." I had never stopped worrying about the conversation I overheard between Mrs. Dimelroot and another teacher while I stood at the drinking fountain. She even brought it up again at the teacher meeting in the library.

Mr. McNulty set his pen down. "Is that still bothering you?"

I nodded.

"Borgia, I am not going to call Child Protective Services. I promise. During the summer I volunteer at your aunt's Animal Shelter. She provides a great service to the community. I know you are safe with her."

I exhaled with relief. In that moment, Mrs. Dimelroot's veiled threats lifted from my heart. School took on a completely different feeling. "Bye, McNut," I said, "See you tomorrow."

"Borgia," Mr. McNulty aimed a yellow pencil at me.

"Yes?"

"One more thing."

I stopped abruptly—right under the green Washington State flag that dangled so low it brushed my face. I was also next to the class set of sweet potato sprouts—28 jars poking up new leaves and tubers leaning toward the sun beams from the window.

"Do you realize how smart you are?" Mr. McNulty tipped his head. "You are one smart kiddo."

"Me?" I brushed the flag out of my eyes.

"Yes, you. You're very intelligent. Sure, you have some catching up to do, but it's obvious you have a fine mind. You can be whatever you want to be." He grinned. "That's all." He turned back to his desk and his pile of student papers. "Say hi to Maya for me," he added without looking up.

I walked home alone that day, enjoying all the sounds of the forest–birds calling as they flitted through the trees, squirrels chittering from high branches. I even admired the sound of jets gliding high in the clouds. The suburbs are not so bad, I told myself. Once I crested the top of the hill, I ran all the way home, knowing that Eightball and all the other dogs would be over-joyed to see me. Home, I had just thought of the shelter as home. I laughed out loud at the idea.

CHAPTER
TWENTY-SEVEN

Mom sent four post cards from Paris. I could barely read her loopy scrawl in faint, silver ink. Maya helped me decipher the words when I got stuck. Mom wrote in cursive, and the glittery gel letters were blurry. Figuring out her words was like trying to solve a jumble puzzle, but I loved the postcards, especially photos of the Eiffel Tower all lit up at night. It was about the only Paris landmark I recognized.

Mom wrote that France was expensive. She shopped at a farmers' market every day and was actually cooking meals to save money. She found a tiny apartment in an area called the Left Bank. Only one burner worked on the stove, and the bed sagged in the middle. There were no curtains on the windows. She said the tiny TV was a joke. However, Paris was beautiful and she felt lucky to be there.

One Saturday Mom actually called, and we talked for ten minutes. "Gluten-free baguettes and croissants are my favorite food, Borgia." She said the French people did not like the way Del spoke French and always corrected him. They complained about his twangy American accent. "His version of French sounds like cowboy lingo to the Parisians, but they love our music. No complaints there."

Mom sent more art postcards–one of the *Mona Lisa* and two pastel–colored bridges by some guy named Monet. At recess I told Kimberly, "My Mom has seen the *Mona Lisa.*" Kimberly was not impressed. She adjusted her pink headband and rolled her eyes, while her friends stared at me skeptically. Kimberly had already been to Paris twice and seen much better. All right, Kimberly, I will never be able to impress you. Before I had time to get huffy and snap some mean comment, Mei Ling grabbed my arm and walked me out to the edge of the playfield. We leaned against the chain link fence and enjoyed some privacy. Mei Ling said one day we would travel to Paris together and speak perfect French, no American accent. She was learning French from an app on her cell phone.

As the weather got warmer and warmer, it became evident I had outgrown all my clothes. Neither my ruby slippers nor my purple boots fit. Maya took me shopping at Nordstroms. She said when she was little, Nordstroms was just a shoe store, but now they sold all kinds of clothing. She bought me two pairs of jeans, four t-shirts and a light rain jacket. I picked out a pair of green and white running shoes for school, and when she saw me admiring a pair of cowboy boots, she bought those too. I wore the boots whenever I rode Bello, and sometimes I wore them to school.

One sunny Saturday I had just pulled on my cowboy boots, when I heard a car coming up our hill. I hurried to my bedroom window and watched as a cherry-colored sports car skidded to a stop in the shelter's driveway.

A young woman slipped out from behind the steering wheel. She wore white-framed sunglasses and red ankle boots that matched her silky blouse. Her dark hair flowed over her shoulders, and her yoga pants accented her slim figure. She held up a cherry red cell phone and immediately began texting. Then she extended the phone at arm's length and snapped some selfies. Even from my upstairs window, I could see her polished nails were light pink with shimmering silver raindrops. Her shoulder bag glittered. Wow, she looked like a fashion model.

I clattered down the back stairs in my new boots and headed down the hall, crashing through the door into the shelter waiting room, just in time to see the stylish young woman point a long fingernail at Eightball, who sat nearby thumping his tail. "That dog belongs to me," she said in a haughty voice. "I can prove it."

The lady's assertion that Eightball belonged to her blotted out all my fabulous first impressions. She instantaneously transformed into an evil witch, a villain. Eightball, apparently appreciating the great interest she took in him, scooted closer and placed a large paw on the toe of her boot. Eager to keep her attention, he thrust his slobbery snout toward her hand. She jumped back quickly and snapped another picture.

"Big mistake," I said breathlessly, rushing to my dog's side. I placed my hand on Eightball's head. "This is my dog. He is a stray and a mutt."

The woman lowered her cell phone to take me in. She did not appear the least perturbed by my words.

"You have the wrong dog kennel," I continued. "If you follow the Y in the road to the left, you come to the Pampered Pets Purebred Spa. I bet that's where your dog is."

The young woman batted her heavily lined eyes and focused on me with a tight-lipped smile.

"You're wrong," she said. "This dog is purebred, a designer breed, my own creation. Look, how much do you want for him? I'll pay you."

"He's not for sale." I folded my arms across my chest. I suddenly felt weak in the knees.

"Every dog has a price, Sweetie, $2000, $5000. I'm sure you could buy any puppy you want for that amount of money." I blanched. Even one thousand dollars was a huge amount. Money would be a great help to the shelter, pay for bags and bags of dog food.

As if she had read my mind she said, "I'll even throw in a donation of $5000 to this animal shelter, or as the sign says, dog pound. How retro. I like it. Reminds me of old movies. Stephen, write that down." Stephen, who had only recently pulled up behind the cherry sports car, in a large black Land Rover, started typing on an iPad. Then he began snapping photos of his own.

Maya, standing behind the counter, was taking it all in. Now she stepped forward. "You have made an error," she said politely. "This dog was dropped off on Christmas Eve by a man in an old pickup truck."

"I know," the lady said. "Ernesto was supposed to be working for me, not against me. I happened to be in the Bahamas for Christmas. The puppies got out of hand. We can only care for a few dogs at my Seattle home, so several were sent out to be boarded. Ernesto took the wrong fork in the road that night. This poor pup got the worst of it, dropped off at this shelter, rather than the Purebred Spa."

"What's his name?" I demanded, believing I could prove her wrong. "The pup arrived with a name. Do you know his name?"

"Certainly." The lady began counting on her fingers. "There were three pups sent to the kennel that night–Sylvia, Tanya and Eightball. Hal, my top trainer, dropped off Sylvia and Tanya at Pampered Purebreds earlier in the day, right before the big snowstorm.

"My maid, Maria, kept the pick of the litter, at the house,

but when he began pulling on the Christmas tree and tried to eat a glass ornament, she decided to board him as well. Our house kennels were full, so she entrusted Eightball to my yard man, Ernesto, who lives out here in the sticks. It was snowing hard. Obviously, he made a wrong turn at the Y in the road. We finally figured it out. Thank heavens, Eightball is here today, looking better than ever, almost exactly like his sisters and brothers, but oh, so much more designer perfection."

The word Eightball had never sounded so terrible. That was the name the truck driver had called out right before he left. I exploded like a firework. I tried to shove the lady, but a man's arm came between me and her silky blouse.

"You can't have Eightball," I screamed. "You left him behind on Christmas Eve. Do you know how terrible it is to be left behind? It was freezing. He was bleeding. You abandoned him." I started to cry, not just for Eightball, but for myself, as all the tragedy of that night returned.

The man from the Range Rover let go of my arm. "Be careful, Susanna," he said. Now I knew this woman's first name.

"No worries," she snapped. "I'm used to uncivilized behavior." Pushing a stray tendril of hair behind her ear, she revealed a sparkling ruby earring, encrusted with emeralds. "Fred, get the leash," she said to a short man in a suit who stepped out of the Range Rover. "Stephen, cut them a check."

"Wait," Maya said. "What proof do you have this is your dog? You can't prove he belongs to you. No paperwork was filled out. This pup was dumped off without identification of any kind. You have no legal right to this animal."

Susanna turned on Maya. "I can prove he is my dog. All my dogs have chips implanted under their skin that will identify me as the legal owner. No official title means he was never legally relinquished to you. I have my attorney with me. Mr. John Dice, to be exact. John, tell these people my rights."

A man with a sour expression, wearing a polka dot bow tie and wire rimmed glasses, appeared on her iPad. Stephen aimed the screen at Maya.

"I have the pup's papers right here in front of me," John Dice said. "Eightball Cavender, born October 24; father, Jemstone, Newfoundland, Black Lab; Mother, Alsta, Newfoundland, Australian Shepherd. Chip number 2888. A vet can prove ownership, if you still want more."

"My designer pup," Susanna chirped. "What did I tell you?" She snapped another photo. "Eightball has by far the best conformation of all the pups. I give you credit, young girl, for taking such good care of him. I'm sure he is gentle, smart and protective—all part of my design. Soon this will be a new AKC breed, and as you can see, this dog is priceless. He will likely become a star at the Westminster Dog Show."

I wrung my hands and started walking backwards, nearly tripping in my new cowboy boots. "Maya, stop her," I mumbled in a strangled voice.

I had to do something. Now! I whistled. Eightball came to me on command, as I ran out the door with him tearing after me. Together, we disappeared into the evergreen forest across the driveway. I could hear shouting behind me, but I had guessed right. None of those fancy rich people were going to run after me into the woods. No one did. Maya, with her bad knees, stayed put too.

TWENTY-EIGHT

I deliberately veered off the main walking path and headed down a partially obscured deer trail that led to the woods back of Remy's barn. I had to duck under brambles and break branches to get through the underbrush. I was eager to reach the hayloft where I had stowed my "running away" kit, if I ever decided to head back to Seattle.

In the backpack were two bottles of water, various granola bars and dry dog food. The hidden emergency stash gave me great comfort, making me believe I could leave the shelter at any time. Remy knew about my "running away" kit. He even added some special bags of almonds and chocolate. He said he would help me if I decided to take off. I had almost forgotten about leaving, now that I had such a busy life. Today I was relieved my stash of supplies was intact. My old wicker suitcase was stowed under the straw. Packed inside were extra clothes and a warm jacket, I had purchased at Value Village.

My eyes stung as I stumbled over roots and rocks. I failed to stop for thorny salmonberry and blackberry bushes that ripped at my arms. When I arrived at Remy's property, the deep shadows of the barn hid me. I looked in the stall where Bello was munching some hay, then hurried up the crude ladder to the loft. Eightball gamely climbed the steps behind me. Once in the loft, he wagged his tail, jumping and romping in the hay, only pausing to sneeze a couple times, then woofing as if inviting me to play.

"Not now, Eightball. This is no joke." Tears streamed down my face. I pulled out my phone and texted Remy.

I'M in the loft with Eightball
    Can you help me?

I PULLED Eightball close and buried my head in his fur. He was overjoyed to get so much attention. His tail thumped in my face. "You are my dog, Eightball. I won't let Susanna steal you."

It took Remy forever to reach the barn. Finally I heard him climbing the ladder, then his head appeared through the hole in the floor. Eightball ran to him and licked his face.

"Cut it out," Remy said, pushing him away. "Borgia, what the heck?"

After hearing the whole story, Remy said, "You can't stay here. I'm sure this is one of the first places they will look."

"What can I do?" I was frantic. "Eightball won't keep quiet or hold still."

"Listen, I hear a car." Remy ran to the barn wall and peeked through a knothole. " It's the police." Eightball started to bark. "Wait here." Remy pulled a couple pieces of beef jerky from his pocket and threw them at me. Then he disappeared down the ladder.

I couldn't stand it. I got up and peered through the knothole. Down below, Mr. Will stood in the driveway next to a black and white police car, talking to two officers. Soon, a Range

Rover and cherry colored sports car zoomed up behind them. Susanna and Stephen got out of their vehicles and joined the officers. How did they know I was here?

I saw Remy point away from the barn, toward the horse pasture then shrug his shoulders. The police walked toward the house. Mr. Will was gesticulating with his hands as he led them onto the front porch. I looked at my phone vibrating like a mad hornet. Maya was texting me.

BORGIA

Come home right now!

I TURNED my phone off and slipped it back in my pocket. Remy stayed in the house for an eternity. The more I tried to contain Eightball, the more he squirmed. I threw my arms around him, and he growled good-naturedly, then romped through the hay, pulling me. Eventually, I got him to lie down. I heard new voices, so peeked out to see Susanna and Stephen walking up the steps of Remy's porch. To my great relief, a few minutes later, they returned to their cars and drove away.

Unfortunately, one of the policemen was pointing at the barn and fiddling with a flashlight. The other officer leaned casually against his car, speaking into a walkie talkie.

Then I heard an officer rummaging around directly below me, right next to Bello's stall. The horse snorted at him questionably and pawed the floor. The sound of clinking bridles and creaking saddles revealed the policeman was right below us in the tack room. Occasionally, his flashlight beamed up through the slats in the loft floor. I hunkered down in my nest of hay. To my great alarm, I now heard someone on the ladder, starting to climb the rungs. I pulled Eightball close to me behind a stack of hay and continued to stuff him full of granola bars.

"Hello," a policeman said, "anybody up here?" Above him in the rafters, pigeons fluttered when he ran his light along the ceiling. As his footsteps scuffled along the floor, I pulled more strands of straw over us and pressed down as flat as possible.

"See anything up there, Joe?" an officer's voice called from below.

"Nothing but hay bales and a few flustered pigeons. I doubt you could get a dog to climb this ladder."

Whew, how wrong he is. Please leave. I was almost out of treats. Eightball was shifting, getting more and more restless. I itched all over. I felt like an old-fashioned scarecrow, with pieces of straw poking out of my clothes.

"We can drive by the elementary school where the boy said she might hide." The officer's flashlight beamed all around me. Only a few bales of hay separated us now.

"Come on down, Joe," the other policeman said. "Let's move on." I held my breath as the flashlight roamed over the rafters directly overhead. Mercifully, the beam started to move away toward the opening in the floor. Remy must have decided to send them on a wild goose chase to my school. Good job!

As I listened to the officer retreating down the ladder, I breathed a sigh of relief. I was out of treats. Eightball was trying to get away from me.

I heard a car door open. They must be leaving. I sat up and listened for the motor. Unfortunately, when the engine revved to life, Eightball started barking. I tried to muzzle him, but he was impossible, obviously tired of hiding, tired of our game. He ducked down, pulled away from me and tore through the hay, disappearing down the hole in the floor. Frantically, I stumbled to the barn wall and stared through a knothole. I watched as my giant pup, covered in strands of alfalfa hay, bounded out the barn door, barking and wagging his tail. Mr. Will and Remy both stepped onto the front porch at the same time.

"Is this the dog we are looking for?" an officer asked, rolling down his window.

"No," Remy yelled.

"Yes," Mr. Will said, nodding.

It was all over within minutes. I stepped out of the barn, covered in hay. A policeman held a car door open, and immediately, Eightball leapt into the back seat. As soon as the door slammed shut, he leaned his muzzle out the half opened window, an excited gleam in his eyes. I began to cry.

After the car sped away, Mr. Will drove me back to the shelter, where I sobbed miserably for hours. Maya could not console me. I only stopped crying when I finally hatched a plan to make a run for it and rescue Eightball.

CHAPTER
TWENTY-NINE

I spent the next week moping, barely eating. I refused to go to school. Maya was beside herself as she tried to reason with me. Only Remy had any positive effect. Since Remy promised to help, Maya let me spend as much time with him as I wanted. He had discovered Susanna's address online. He showed me pictures of every room in her huge house and the layout of her property. There was even a photo of her dog kennels behind an aquamarine swimming pool.

"She must be rich," I said, "like dripping with pool water rich. How do you know so much about her house anyway, Remy?"

"Because," he said proudly, "Susanna happens to live in the same neighborhood as my private school. Her residence is inside an exclusive, gated community called Brickhaven. It's like old, old Seattle families, and yeah really wealthy."

On the computer screen, Susanna's home looked gigantic, two brick chimneys, numerous gables. Her lawn was bordered by clipped hedges with big shade trees in the front. Mom had mislead me to believe all rich people lived on the east side of the lake. Apparently, not true.

"Susanna's house borders the golf course," Remy said.

"Good to know, but I need a plan." I was staring at a printed map of the surrounding neighborhood.

Remy wanted to move slowly, but I was not going to wait much longer. I had recently restocked all the supplies of my running away kit in the barn. Now as I studied a map of the Tolt Pipeline trail, I noted the path ran west toward Seattle. On my dog walks, at the crest of the hill, I always searched for the Space Needle and the high-rise buildings of the city outlined on the horizon—close enough to be in plain sight. My goal was in reach. I could walk to Susanna's. Then Remy shared my plans with Lump and reported back that if I waited one more month, he would have his car finished and could drive me there. I certainly did not want to wait a month. I could not stand to wait another week.

Reluctantly, I returned to school. I was not focusing on my lessons or paying attention in class. I barely touched my lunch. Mei Ling said I wasn't as much fun. I never answered the notes she passed to me, and she could no longer make me laugh. Mr. McNulty even called me in at recess and asked me what was wrong.

Maya knew why I was upset. She tried her best to help me by contacting Susanna, who did not return calls or answer texts. All I could think about was Eightball. I needed to get him back before he was sold or sent far away.

I spent most of my time talking to Remy about running away. To do that, I had to spend time with his flying contraptions. I got used to turning round and round, following their whirring paths in the sky.

"Plane or drone?" I asked, squinting up at the clouds.

"Drone," Remy said, not bothering to look.

Remy's mind was surprising. It took off in all directions, just like his flying machines. "You can get Eightball back," he said, as he examined downed pieces of metal that had crashed on the grass. "I have more information."

When we got back to the basement, Remy cleared a space on his workbench and unfolded a map of the area he had found buried in his dad's desk. Using a sharpie, he drew a line from Maya's shelter, creating a route that followed the Tolt Pipeline Trail and headed toward Seattle. Then he marked streets along the route. "I'm choosing the ones that have less traffic, and these walking paths are along old railroad lines connected to several parks."

"I want to go right away," I said, frantically. "I can follow that map."

"I was trying to show you how far it is to walk," Remy said, scratching his head. "At least a couple days just to reach the Floating Bridge over the lake. I suppose you could take a bus, but better yet, remember Lump will have his car completed soon. It's almost ready."

I crossed my arms and tapped my foot. I hated waiting. Somehow, I managed to rein in my sharp tongue, while Remy jabbered on with tons of details, reminding me more and more of his dad, Mr. Will.

"Here's a lucky feature," Remy said. "Note the floating bridge spans Lake Washington." He moved his sharpie across it. "Susanna lives off this first exit after crossing the water." He marked an X on her home then drew a big circle. "This is some of the least developed land in all of Seattle. It belongs to the University of Washington."

Apparently Susanna's house was surrounded by a huge nature preserve and a golf course. He drew his hand dramatically through the air. "Acres and acres of empty land. Wait, it gets better. The university planted trees there from all over the world. It's called the Arboretum, and it borders Susanna's neighborhood where huge houses stand behind a security entrance with guards."

"We will never get through a secured fence with guards."

"Oh yeah, we can! I know where there's a hole in the fence and the guards are mostly at the main gate. We can squeeze through the hole and get onto the golf course without anyone seeing us."

"How do you know all this information, Remy?"

"My school is nearby. I've spent hours running around the Arboretum, up and down the paths through the trees. The nature preserve is open to the public, and best of all, it shares a fence with Susanna's private neighborhood. Promise not to tell, and I will share a secret."

" Promise not to tell what?" Remy's long explanation was making me fidgety.

"My friend Clancy and I discovered the hole in the fence by chance. We squeezed through it directly onto the golf course and spent hours exploring the fairways."

"What's a fairway?" I knew nothing about golf.

"The acres of grass where golf balls land after they are hit. The game of golf has 18 holes of park-like grass. Golfers walk up and down the fairways or drive in carts, then try to hit their golf balls into a tiny hole with a flag. People dress in crazy outfits and clomp around in cleated shoes. Look."

He pointed to a spot on the map. "Clancy and I built a tree house in this fir tree on the 9th hole. Quite a view up there, especially when stray balls veer off course into the forest. After golfers give up on lost balls, we find them. Hunting golf balls is better than hunting Easter Eggs. The pro shop buys them back for a $1 each. That's a lot of candy bars and soda."

So much for old memories, I wanted to plan our route. "Are

you telling me you can get us into the gated community by squeezing through a hole in a fence?"

"Righto," Remy said.

"Show me where Susanna lives again." I peered at the map.

Remy drew a circle around Susanna's house, but then marked a red X on the hole location. "The fence hole is right here behind a huge compost pile that steams. It's so stinky, no sane human goes near it. Once through the fence, cross the fairway and bingo we arrive at Susanna's house."

I did not plan to climb any trees, but I indulged Remy, as he marked an X on the spot where his tree house was located.

"I don't understand how you have so much free time to run around a golf course when you are supposed to be at school."

"The school is a long way from our homes across Lake Washington. Sometimes Clancy and I wait hours for our parents to get off work, and pick us up. We use the time to play outdoors, explore the arboretum, the golf course, and plug coins into the candy machines at the pro shop. We have a ball—hah, hah—golf ball, that is. Our parents think we are studying in the library. Mom would kill me if she knew how much goofing around I do, how many chocolate bars I devour."

I sighed. Remy was focused on old memories. I think he saw the frustration in my eyes.

"Look," he said, trying to keep my attention. "I have been examining the Floating Bridge schedule. In a few weeks the bridge will close all night for repairs. Traffic is prohibited beginning at dusk. The bridge does not open again until six in the morning. We need to make sure Lump drives you when the bridge is open, not closed." I agreed. Remy printed the bridge schedule and posted it on his bulletin board.

My mind was spinning. Lump could not drive me on a closed bridge, but I could ride Bello when there were no cars. If

Lump didn't hurry up, I just might go it alone on a horse. Lump was in high school, so most of his work on the driverless car took place on weekends. Sometimes when I thought he was working, he was playing video games. Twice I happened upon him napping on the couch. I began to think he would never get his car in working order.

As time passed, riding Bello seemed the best plan. Bello was such a calm, steady horse. He could handle streets and traffic. Remy said he had been in parades and was not the least afraid of cars. Now that he had rubber shoes to protect his hooves from asphalt, it seemed much more reasonable.

If I rode the horse across the bridge, I could rescue Eightball myself. I even hatched a crazy plan to offer the diamond tiara to Susanna as payment for her designer dog. I knew Susanna liked bling. I carefully wrapped up the sparkling crown and stowed it in my backpack. The more I looked at it, the more I wondered if the diamonds were real. Too upsetting to think about. Mom had mentioned stolen jewelry. The princess lady on the yacht gave me the tiara, didn't she? I pushed it out of my mind and switched to my solo plan. I wanted some lights for Bello's safety in the dark. In a box of decorations in the closet of my bedroom, I found the perfect string of battery-operated lights that I could drape around his saddle.

I was annoyed with Lump and Remy. They treated my rescue plan like a fantasy, like a video game. Often, they were talking about motors and flight patterns, when I wanted to talk about crossing the bridge and following the route to Susanna's home.

One evening after I caught Lump once again napping on the couch, I cemented my decision. I told Remy I could not wait any longer. Lump told me to relax. There was no hurry. Remy agreed. The boys wanted me to look at maps and plot a course. They did not think I had any proof that Eightball was actually at Susanna's. They said call and find out for sure. Remy offered to fly a drone over the house and look from above, but somehow, he never did. Susanna had not answered any of Maya's calls. I left the two cousins in the basement and stormed upstairs. As far as I was concerned, I was on my own. I had to take action. It was now or never.

THIRTY

I had been riding Bello for months. I could bridle him, even manage the saddle, but only the light English one Remy used when going over jumps. I knew what the big horse ate, drank and how to cool him down when he got overheated. I could do this.

I went over Remy's drawings. The Tolt Pipeline Trail, where Maya and I walked the dogs, was my first route of escape. From there, I would connect to the old railroad lines now transformed into walking trails.

Smack in the middle of my route stood Bridle Trails Park, over 600 acres of horse-friendly paths, bordered by homes with barns and pastures. This neighborhood was filled with horses, meaning I would not look out of place riding a horse. Water troughs were everywhere. I bet I could even score some hay. Bridle Trails Park allowed no cars, not even bicycles. The whole park was focused around equestrian activity.

The worst part of my journey was to cross the huge floating bridge across Lake Washington, but it would not be so bad if the span was closed to traffic. After checking the closure schedule pinned to Remy's bulletin board, I knew the bridge shutdown would happen in the next few days.

I decided to leave Remy out of the plan. I was afraid he would never let me take Bello and go it alone. On the morning of my big escape, I waved good-bye to Maya, who thought I was on my way to school. Instead, I scrambled down the foot trail to Remy's barn. Bello snorted eagerly when he saw me.

Once in the saddle, my backpack secure, we headed to our first route, the Tolt Pipeline. Bello sauntered at a pleasant walk, whisking his tail from side to side as we moved up and down the hills toward Lake Washington. I felt at home on this familiar trail. I had walked various segments of this pipeline path many times with Maya and her leashed dogs. I paused for a moment at the crest of the hill and saluted the ghostly outline of the Space Needle on the horizon. Home was glimmering at me. I patted Bello's neck. I loved everything about this horse, the creak of the leather saddle, the clop of his hooves, even the sweet smell of his scent. With Bello, I could rescue Eightball.

Finding the old railroad tracks, the next leg of my journey was more difficult. The tracks had long ago been converted into walking paths. Some of them were paved and not horse friendly. People were out walking with dogs. Bicycles buzzed by, going way too fast. I did not encounter anyone else on horseback, but no one seemed to mind that I was there.

When I finally reached the entrance to Bridle Trails State Park, I breathed a huge sigh of relief. The park was amazing—miles and miles of dirt trails specifically for horses, in dense forests among towering evergreen trees. I led Bello under some huge fir trees and let him drink his fill from a public watering trough. Then he leaned over a fence and joined two other horses, sharing their crunchy alfalfa hay. So far, all was going well. No one had given me any trouble. After resting for an hour and studying my map, we headed out again toward another park in a community right next to the longest floating bridge in the world.

By the time I reached the lakefront neighborhood, I was starting to feel saddle sore. According to a digital sign, the bridge did not close for several hours, so I reined Bello in and stopped to look around. The local park was crowded with people and dogs. Children ran over the lawns past a large duck pond. I watched for a few minutes, then urged Bello forward and rode up and down the tree lined streets, hoping to look inconspicuous.

Most adults stayed clear of me, but an elderly lady walked by with a fat beagle tugging on his leash. "What a pretty horse," the lady said. I thanked her and hoped horses were not unusual in this neighborhood. A few blocks further, I happened on a horse pasture with a young woman riding in circles on a golden palomino. I also noted two girls in knee high leather boots, on fat ponies, both riding English style. Grateful for the other horses, I told myself, "Hang in there just make it across the bridge." I was grimy and hungry, beginning to feel somewhat guilty for taking this gentle horse from his safe pasture and nightly oat mash.

As evening approached, I was having a hard time keeping Bello's head up. He was hungry and kept trying to sample the flowers, even the shrubs. Just then, my cell phone lit up in the plastic bag dangling from my saddle. The sound was turned off, but the vibration made its own demands. I managed to extract the phone and get it up to my ear, all the while tugging on Bello's reins as he devoured clumps of greenery.

"Hi Remy," I said, trying to sound as casual as possible.

"Borgia, are you crazy? Have you lost your mind?" Remy sounded irritated, like his voice had been run through a cheese grater.

"On track to rescue Eightball, just like we planned."

"Not like we planned. Where are you? Are you on Bello?"

"Yeah. I am in a neighborhood park, in a suburb. Anyway, the park you showed me on the map, the one closest to the Floating Bridge. I am looking at a duck pond. Hold on. Bello keeps eating flowers." I jerked hard on the reins and pulled Bello's head up. He had a pink rosebud dangling from his mouth. I guided him back to the sidewalk where there was nothing to eat.

"Borgia, put your ear bud in so you don't have to use your hands."

"Good idea." I fished in my pocket and pulled out the white cords. "Found it, Can you hear me?"

"Yeah, I hear you. What the heck is going on."

"I told you. I am waiting for the bridge to close, then ride Bello across the lake, take the Arboretum exit, just like you instructed me. You said you didn't want to come with me, so...."

Remy interrupted me. "Lump was going to drive you. I can't believe you took off on a horse."

"Lump had so many delays. His car had a flat tire; it needed oil and all those naps on your sofa. I couldn't wait any longer. I plan to be back with Eightball by tomorrow. I followed your route."

"Borgia, you're crazy. I am worried. Keep your phone on."

"I will," I said, but Remy had already hung up. He sounded beyond upset.

The sun was sinking. The sky was lovely shades of pink and orange. An eerie quiet settled over the park. The last of the dog walkers and children disappeared. I was hungry. I scarfed down a granola bar and drank some water. My legs ached from sitting so long in the saddle.

When the sun finally blazed its most brilliant pink, it set off the dark silhouettes of high rise buildings on the other side of the lake. 'Bridge Closed' the sign now said. It was time to cross.

Bello and I made our way to the freeway entrance. A huge sign straddling the on-ramp said, "STOP! CLOSURE." I checked the battery-powered lights that were wound around the saddle to use only if needed. Ignoring the sign, Bello and I headed onto the bridge.

I now noted half way across there was a lighted guard tower. Remy had not alerted me to this barrier. Below the tower, two men were moving about in reflective vests. As I watched, they began to set out traffic cones and string orange, plastic webbing across the lanes. As I drew closer to the barricade, a burly man appeared, standing smack in the middle of the bridge, brandishing a flashlight like a light saber.

At that moment, my phone began jangling, vibrating against my leg. I couldn't answer. I could barely hold on to my resolve and keep going. Bello snorted. I pulled him in from a brisk trot and tried to think. The burly man was blowing a whistle. I could barely hear its faint, tweet, tweet. Two men in hardhats were standing next to the orange plastic webbing and waving their hands in the air as if to discourage me. Obviously, I had been discovered, probably by security cameras. I had to decide whether to continue or abandon hope and turn back.

THIRTY-ONE

When I saw the guard standing dead center on the bridge and the construction hardhat guys holding up a makeshift barricade, an image of Eightball struck. I pictured the frantic pup with blood dripping from his mouth as he fought to escape his cage in the middle of a snowstorm, the same snowstorm I was in too.

With that image before me, no doubt remained. I clamped my legs and pressed my heels into Bello's side, urging him into a gentle canter. I was careful to keep my feet securely in the stirrups just like Remy had taught me. Bello arched his neck as if for battle. My hair flew out behind me. I felt the cool breeze from the lake. Lights were popping on all around us.

Upon drawing closer, I realized that the barricades were made out of the same orange netting as the jumps in Remy's pasture. Plus the bridge ones were not nearly as high. I was grateful. How often Remy had told me Bello was the calmest horse he had ever ridden–unfazed by traffic and lights. Hopefully, he would be unfazed by yelling bridge guards. I could now detect the anger in their faces.

When we were almost upon them, I dug my heels into

Bello's side and urged him faster into a gallop. I had a good hold on the reins and even part of his mane, as I leaned over his neck. Even though he was wearing his rubber shoes, his hooves rang on the asphalt, a strange clattering music

The men were yelling. The heavyset man in the center held his arm straight in the air and shouted, "Halt!" I kept my eyes riveted straight ahead, ignoring the shouting. But now the heavyset man was waving a flashlight in my eyes. Thank heavens Bello loved to jump. Effortlessly, we were up and over the orange webbing and galloping down the center lane of the world's largest Floating Bridge as if there had been no barriers at all.

I did not glance back. I could still hear the men yelling. Ignore them, I told myself. Look straight ahead. Stay focused. Cold spray from the waves slapped the side of the bridge and pelted my face. In the distance, Seattle's familiar city lights beckoned.

For a few seconds, I was completely alone. Then a car motor sounded directly behind me, and a voice boomed over a loud-speaker. Bello shied and hopped sideways. I almost fell off, slipped down over the saddle, but quickly righted myself as I still had a tight grip on his long mane.

"Whoa," I said, talking to Bello. "Easy, easy." My heart pounded as a sea-green Fiat drove alongside us. It was defi-nitely the car I had stared at for so many days, hoping Lump and Remy would get it running.

"Lump," I shouted as a window lowered. "Lump, Is that you?"

"No," the voice said, coming from inside the car. "It's me, Remy."

"Remy?" I was puzzled.

"Borgia, there's no time to waste. Why haven't you answered your phone?" I could hardly speak as I bounced in the saddle at a fast trot, trying to keep an even pace with the little car.

"I can't ride and talk. My ear buds fell out. I'm trying to stay on this horse and make it across the bridge."

"Can you put the earbuds back in?

"Not right now, they are dangling around my neck."

"Ok," Remy said. " I can hear you just fine from the speaker in the car, so it may not matter."

"Remy? Is it really you? I can't see you in there. It's so dark."

"Yeah, it's me. Look, it has to appear I have taken custody of you. Hop off Bello and hook his bridle to the rope in the back. Then get in the car."

"What? Are you nuts?" Just then the bridge flooded with more lights.

"Borgia, trust me. We have to work together. Only a couple minutes before adults descend on us. There are all kinds of security folks conferring on computers right now, trying to figure out who you are, who I am. We only have minutes before they come after us. Believe me, there are cameras everywhere on this bridge."

"All right," I said, and eased down from the saddle. When Remy ground to a halt, I clipped Bello's bridle to the thick rope dangling from the bumper. Pulling open the passenger door, I fell into the front seat. To my surprise, the driver seat was empty. I panicked. "Remy, where are you? You know I can't drive a car."

Remy's voice crackled from the dashboard. "Don't worry, Borgia. I am driving, but remotely, like I fly my drones. Lump cobbled together a driverless car, remember? Relax, we are almost across the bridge, almost to Susanna's."

"Are you at home?"

"Yep, in the basement. Look, Lump is going to pick you up in his uncle's truck with a horse trailer attached. Drive you and

Bello back. We have it all arranged. He will drive around the end of the lake since the bridge is closed."

I collapsed against the seat. The window went up, and the sea-green car continued slowly over the empty bridge, with Bello trotting cheerfully behind. I stared over the edge at the inky water. Across the lake, the lights of the city glimmered.

"Lump and I worked on the remote car together," Remy's staticky voice was chattering away. "If I can fly a plane from the basement, I can certainly drive a car."

"I'm nervous, Remy." I had never ridden in a driverless car before.

"Hold on. We have to make it down this exit and get off the bridge. I am going to dodge the barricades. Once the security folks coordinate their information, they will send the police." As he spoke, the little car swerved and zigzagged through an array of barrels and cones.

Tossed from side to side, it felt like a wild ride at the fair. "Careful of Bello," I screamed. "This is not a video game, Remy."

"Bello's fine," Remy said in his calm voice. "I can see him in my rear camera. He's doing better than you are. I am going really slow for him."

"Land ho," he yelled triumphantly, and the car veered around a big 'STOP! WRONG WAY' sign. Over the exit ramp, at the edge of the lake, lay a thick swamp of cattails poking up from murky water, only visible because of a bright moon that had suddenly appeared in the sky.

"Welcome to the University of Washington Arboretum," Remy exclaimed. He sounded like a tour guide. "It's mercifully dark, except for the moon and one or two streetlights. I hope no one saw me take that wrong way exit, but who's kidding who? Cameras are everywhere. At least maybe some are turned off due to the repairs, and I know the arboretum will be dark in most spots."

"Spooky," I muttered, twisting my hands together as I stared out the window at the shadowy trees. "I like lights. The city is always brimming with lights."

"The dark is saving our skins," Remy insisted. "No cameras, and the moon and stars are too far away to reveal us. It's our big chance. My school is only a few blocks from here. We practice soccer in the field to your right. My robotic class flies drones in that grass meadow. Do you see a spiked gate?"

"I see an iron barrier. Is that it?"

"Yep. Behind that big gate is Susanna's house. Hopefully the dark continues to hide us. Hardly any light now that the moon has gone behind a cloud."

The little car wound along the lakeshore, under a pitch-black sky. "Trees from all over the world," Remy kept reminding me, as if I would never appreciate that fact. Shadowy lawns and gardens ran under the trees, rolling right down to the water. A streetlight near a pond illuminated lily pads and sleeping ducks on logs, their beaks tucked under their feathers. Just as we turned onto a dirt road and were completely enveloped by the dark, sirens screamed.

CHAPTER

THIRTY-TWO

"We better split up," Remy said. "I'm going to drive to a university parking lot and leave the car there."

"Can we still chat by cell phone then?" I liked hearing Remy's voice. It was much better to have a partner.

"Yep, time to ditch the Fiat, but I'll get back in touch. Keep your ear buds in."

"Got it." I slipped out of the car and unclipped Bello's lead. For a few moments, I leaned against his sweet-smelling neck, taking deep breaths of his wonderful scent. "You are my hero, Bello." His coat was covered with dried sweat, but he was quite calm. I rubbed his velvet muzzle.

My cell buzzed.

"Are you there, Borgia?" Remy asked.

"I'm here," I muttered, but I only felt half present. I was exhausted and filthy, my hair matted, my face grimy. My legs felt so wobbly, I wanted to lie down and rest.

I continued to bury my face in Bello's mane. "I wish you were actually here, Remy."

"Sorry, Borgia. The biggest risk I have ever taken was to run around the golf course, when I was supposed to be studying. Unlike you, I've never had to fend for myself. Confronting Susanna sounds way too stressful."

"I'll confront Susanna. You can offer directions. Please catch a ride with Lump, and help me navigate the golf course. You know it by heart." I waited hopefully, but Remy did not respond.

"Has Lump left yet? I'm really glad he's coming to pick up Bello."

"Nope. He's behind me on the sofa eating a ham sandwich."

"Perfect! So after you park the Fiat, hop in the truck with Lump and join me. You told me the route around the north end of the lake to the University Horticulture Center is only about half an hour if traffic is light. It will take me at least that long to reach that spot where Lump intends to park."

"I don't think I can manage it," Remy said.

Just then a huge, winged creature emerged from the shadow only inches from my face. I screamed. Bello shied. We both jumped.

"What's happening?" Remy yelled. "Are you okay?"

"I don't know. I can't see." I ducked away from the low flying creature, maybe an owl or a bat. Bello tugged at his rope lead. "It's OK, Bello."

"You are worrying me, Borgia. I'll stay on the phone, make sure you find the gravel service road that runs along the lake and leads to the parking lot where Lump will be waiting to load Bello. May take you quite a while to get there."

"Right." I pulled myself back into the saddle and rode cautiously forward, under the dark trees.

"Do you see a curved foot bridge yet?" Remy asked.

"Maybe." I peered through the dark, trying to focus shadows into shapes.

"When you reach the bridge, hop off and lead Bello over it, just in case its hollow sound spooks him."

Bello did not seem to mind the clop of his hooves on the bridge, but I was afraid someone else might hear us. I paused and listened. No one seemed to be there except roosting ducks at the water's edge. The watery moonlight kept coming and going behind clouds.

"You are on the UW horticulture campus now, Remy said, "acres of wild grass land. You may run into some night patrols, mostly college students hired to putt around in golf carts. The kids are notorious for taking it easy. They get bored and goof off, doing wheelies and tricks. Tell me what you can see."

"Glowing greenhouses full of plants, the only buildings with lights."

"Have you reached a downed cedar tree, cut into giant rounds?"

"No, but I smell the scent of cedar. OK, there are the rounds. Crazy dark out here."

"Nice, huh? The police are chasing the car up on the main University of Washington campus. I parked the Fiat near the fountain. Hopefully, the police will think the car is some fraternity prank and leave it alone. Can you still hear sirens?"

I looked up. A helicopter was whirring overhead, flashing red and yellow lights. I guess I wasn't that far from Remy's car. The main University of Washington campus sat right above me on the hill.

"Helicopter above the car now," Remy said breathlessly. "Turning off the engine on the count of three. One, Two...."

"Remy, are you all right?"

"I'll contact you on my cell phone in a few minutes. Gotta go."

I had really slowed down, so stopped for a while, leaning against a huge boulder, and allowed Bello to graze in a grassy area. I was so tired my head drooped. I couldn't keep my eyes open. Soon, I drifted off to sleep. The horse munching grass at the end of his rope became a peaceful sound in my dreams. I don't know how long I was asleep, when Remy's voice startled me awake.

"Borgia, You there?"

"I'm here," I said, rubbing my eyes. " I've been taking a break. Nice little nap. Bello munched on the grass."

" So ready to start walking again. Stay on the gravel road."

"OK," I stretched, but still had hold of Bello's lead. Overhead, I could see the bright lights of high-rise student dorms. Fortunately, Bello and I remained deep in shadow on this UW garden land. I was so stiff, that my legs cramped. Finally, after what felt like hours, I led Bello over the last footbridge and spied Lump's white truck in the empty parking lot. His driver side window was open, so I waved to him. To my amazement, the passenger door flew open and out popped Remy.

"Remy," I shouted, throwing my arms around him. "I hoped you would come."

"Whoa, you are covered in grime." Remy grinned, then looked sheepishly down at his feet. "I can do this, right? Be as brave as you?"

"Duh," I said.

"How about you get the horse in the trailer?" Lump said, watching us from an open window.

Remy took the rope and patted Bello. Unfortunately, Bello tossed his head and lay his ears flat against his head. He did not like the idea of the trailer and balked at going up the ramp. In final protest he pulled his lips back, revealing stained teeth, then let out a shrill whinny. A bag of oats finally persuaded him to climb up the metal ramp into the trailer, where Remy quickly closed the tailgate.

"How about I just wait here?" Lump said. "It's a good

parking spot with no police activity. You guys can retrace your path along the lakeshore, to reach Susanna's, right?" Remy nodded. We had a plan.

CHAPTER

THIRTY-THREE

A s we set off walking along the gravel road, I was happy to have Remy beside me, even if he seemed a bit annoyed. I had been riding horseback way too long and was stiff, but it still felt good to move my legs.

"Maya is beside herself with worry," Remy said, scolding me. "I told her you will be okay, but you should have been more patient, Borgia." I did not respond. Remy was right. I should have waited, but I had also done pretty well by myself.

"Hey, I just remembered," Remy broke into my thoughts, " I know a shortcut along the lake that leads us back into the Arboretum."

He turned sharply, walked down stairs to a dock and headed out on a series of wooden planks built right over the water. The planks crisscrossed through a murky swamp of reeds and lily pads. I admired the shimmering reflections and lights of the city near by. Ducks roosted on logs and mud flats right below us. Some of them lifted their beaks when we passed. Occasionally a frog croaked.

In very short order, we were back on solid ground headed down an arboretum path through the trees. Up ahead, Remy pointed out the shadowy hills of the golf course secure behind a sturdy fence. Suddenly he turned and walked directly into the thick brush, where he pointed out a huge pile of composting vegetation.

"Stinky huh?" he said, pretending to gag. I held my nose as he gallantly held back branches to keep them from snapping in my face. "Doesn't seem like a trail, but works for coyotes and raccoons. "Entry point to Susanna's neighborhood coming right up," he said, getting down on his knees and triumphantly pointing to an opening in the fence. Next he demonstrated how to squeeze through it. I made it easily. We were now inside the gated community and walking along the country club golf course. Ahead, a shadowy pole with a droopy flag marked the spot where the golf balls were supposed to land. Huge houses with glowing windows loomed on the edge of the fairways. Fortunately, tall fir trees also provided us lots of cover.

After walking up and down some gentle inclines, Remy announced, "we have to cross the open fairway here." Stepping from the shadows, we traipsed cautiously across what appeared to be a park- like stretch of lawn. A flag fluttered in the distance, lit by Remy's cell phone.

"Tenth hole," he said. "OK, turn here." But just then a search light lit up the spot. We dropped over the side of the putting green into a pile of sand.

"What the heck is this?" I cried, sinking ankle deep.

" Sand trap," Remy said. "Part of the game. No golfer wants a ball to land here." I could see why not. Moments later we took off again, staying in the shadows .

A beam of light cut through the forest, running over the tree trunks and sword ferns. It almost caught us in its white beam, but Remy dropped to the ground behind a downed maple tree, and I braced myself behind a giant cedar trunk, breathing in its pungent aroma. Finally the search light moved on, roaming over the golf course, illuminating dips and rises in the grass. Raucous music emanated from the little cart, ransacking the silence. The tinny music was paired with the cheerful putt-putt of the cart as it bumped along over the uneven ground.

Remy watched the golf cart moving farther and farther away. "Our chance now," he said. "The patrol guys are pretty lame security." I nodded. We moved on without being detected. Moments later Remy pointed to squares of light.

"Look! There it is—Susanna's house, just like the online photos."

"Hopefully, Eightball is there," I muttered, as we covered the last steps at a brisk walk, careful of holes and divots made by golf clubs. I bit my lip. We were about to trespass onto Susanna's property. As we approached the closed gate at her driveway, a sign posted on a brick wall read VIDEO MONI-TORED 24 HOURS A DAY.

"Maybe it is and maybe it isn't," Remy said. He motioned me to follow him along a neighbor's hedge that separated the driveways. We ducked down and crawled.

The neighbor's hedge was so thick, we could not return to Susanna's property. A fence enclosed her backyard. Remy gave me a leg up, and somehow I managed to climb over it and drop safely onto the lawn. Then he jumped down beside me. A dog in a nearby kennel saw us and wagged its tail. Eightball? No, when my cell light shined on the pup, I saw it was a golden retriever wearing a blue collar. The dog grabbed a rubber ball, dropped it through the kennel wire and looked at us eagerly, cocking its head. Not a watch dog, I guess. When we did not respond, he woofed to get our attention.

"Shhh," I said, holding my finger to my lips. I threw the ball back into his cage, where the pup pounced on it. A twinge of disappointment hit. What if Eightball was not here? Up ahead, Remy was motioning me to follow him down a stone path that curved toward the gigantic house. A swimming pool with underwater lights glimmered next to floor-to-ceiling picture windows. Through the glass slider, a young woman was curled up on a sofa, her face bent intently over the soft light of her phone. In the background a TV flickered, and then I saw a large black dog stretched out in the middle of the room.

"Remy! Eightball." I grabbed his hand and punched him in the shoulder. Just them the dog raised its head and stood up as if it sensed us. To my dismay the animal was much smaller than Eightball. My mood plunged recklessly. Remy frowned when he saw my shoulders slump.

"Not Eightball?" he whispered.

"No!" I sounded like I was going to cry.

"What next?" He shifted one foot to another, as if he had stepped in nettles.

I had no idea. My plan had been to discover Eightball and immediately head back to the shelter. If he was somewhere in this huge house, I would have to confront Susanna, but I could see this was not Susanna. This was, this was.... I knew I had seen this lady before.

" Go round front and ring the doorbell," I said, turning to Remy. "I'll try to sneak through that back door near the garage."

Remy shook his head. "That door is certainly locked, Borgia. I won't know what to say to whoever answers the front door. Is that Susanna on the couch?"

"No, no it's not. She looks kind of like Susanna. Maybe Susanna is in another room." I felt suddenly foolish. But I was desperate, too. Remy looked worried.

"I'll ring the front doorbell," I said, putting my hands on my hips. "You stay here. Wait for me in the bushes. Could you at least try the back door? My mom never locks our doors."

Remy nodded then crept forward, tried to budge the back door, then high-tailed it back without being seen.

"Locked," he said, looking at once triumphant, but also a bit defeated. I left for the front of the house and glanced back at him standing in the rhododendron bushes. Green leaves brushed his face and clumps of red cedar bark clung to the sides of his sneakers. Remy was right again. Only Mom would leave her doors unlocked. He glanced up at me and pointed to his phone to let me know he would text me.

When I reached the front porch, I made a snap decision, unzipped my backpack and placed the diamond tiara on my head. My hands were shaking, my mind speeding. I planned to offer this crown as payment to Susanna, who obviously loved bling. "Trade you Eightball for diamonds," I planned to say. Unfortunately, when the front door opened it was not Susanna, but Maria, the maid Susanna had mentioned, left in charge of the pups when she was gone. Her apron was embroidered with her name in red thread.

"We do not accept solicitations," she said, pointing to a sign over the door. "We don't want to buy anything." She stared at my crown.

"I am not selling anything," I said, squaring my chin. "I want to talk to Susanna."

"Who is it, Maria?" a voice called from the next room.

"A young girl who wants to talk to Susanna," Maria called over her shoulder. Turning back to me, she said quite calmly, "Susanna is not here. She is in Europe."

I felt all my plans collapsing around me like a house of cards. My voice quavered. "I want to see Eightball." I wrinkled my nose to keep from bursting into tears. Maria's forehead furrowed, and she shook her head as if I was asking for something crazy.

"What girl?" The woman's voice sounded more clear as she drew nearer to us. I looked away from the maid's stern face and focused on a blue vase full of red flowers next to a grandfather clock that ticked peacefully near a curving staircase.

A slender woman appeared behind Maria, definitely not Susanna, but I recognized her. We both gasped at the same time. Maria looked from me to her and muttered something in exasperated Spanish. Then she wiped her hands on her apron, and disappeared down the hall.

"My missing tiara," the young woman exclaimed, clasping her hand over her mouth. "The missing diamonds!"

I put my hand to my head and touched the pointy crown. "You gave this to me." I recognized the woman from the Christmas yacht, the beautiful woman with the dark hair who gave me the maraschino cherry from her drink.

"The girl in the Esmeralda costume?" the woman said in surprise, "Your hair was black at the holiday party."

"Temporary dye," I ran my fingers through my grimy hair. Underneath the tiara, it was a tangled mess. "I'm Borgia, and this is my real hair color."

"Of course, Borgia, now I remember." The woman held up a slim hand with golden rings that sparkled. "That night, I was so tired. We both needed a nap." She smiled as she recalled the evening in a dreamy voice. "Swan pillows, a golden coverlet. You wore a red parka, but you say I gave you the tiara? I don't remember that. Wait, I put it on your head, said you were the real princess. I think maybe you are right."

"You said the crown should belong to me," I reminded her. "I liked it, but it was too sharp. You fell asleep, so I put it in my wicker suitcase. I didn't want to hurt your feelings. Then I fell asleep." I stepped on my left foot and teetered nervously.

The woman's face broke into a wide grin. "All this time I thought your mother took it. My bad." She pretended to slap her cheek and laughed. "I guess it was my fault the diamonds disappeared after all."

"The diamonds are real?"

"Very real." The woman gently touched the tiara. "Paul was sure he would never see it again. The tiara belonged to his grandmother in England." I did not really care about Paul and wanted to change the subject.

"Is this Susanna's home?" I only had one thing on my mind. I peered behind her.

"Yes. Do you know my sister Susanna?"

I hesitated. I didn't know what to say. "She took my dog, Eightball, the big black pup."

"Are you the girl from the shelter, that old-fashioned dog pound?"

I nodded. "Susanna told me about you. She probably forgot all about it by now." Just then Remy rounded the corner of the house, both hands stuffed deep in his pockets. "Who's this?" the lady asked.

"I'm Remy," he said, " a friend trying to help Borgia locate her dog."

"Claire," the lady said, stepping forward and extending her hand.

Remy shook her hand, then stepped back and glanced awkwardly at his feet.

"Maria, who's at the door?" An elderly man's voice now called from the hallway.

"Nobody," Maria yelled from a back room. "A girl in a costume trying to sell something."

"I am not selling anything," I said petulantly. An old man now shuffled into view and stood behind Claire in the entryway. He was wearing a frayed blue sweater with chipped, brown buttons. His eyes drooped. His white mustache drooped. His wavy hair looked like it might have once been black. His face softened as he bent over and caught a better glimpse of me.

"Why, hello," he said. "Are you a friend of Susanna's, a neighbor perhaps?"

"Uh, no, I am here to pick up my dog."

"Ohhhh," the man said, as if considering what that meant. He pulled on his mustache thoughtfully. "Susanna has so many dogs. Good to have one leave, but I believe we only have two here right now."

"Papa," Claire said. "Look, the lost tiara." She pointed at my head. "Paul's missing diamonds, the ones he has been fretting over since they disappeared on his yacht last Christmas."

The old man did not look at the tiara or the diamonds. Instead, he looked at Claire. Then he looked at me. "My daughters," he said, throwing up his hands, "are quite spoiled. Diamonds, designer dogs. Is that your crown?" He pointed to my head.

"No, but Claire said it was mine. She placed it on my head at the holiday party on the big white boat and said I should have it."

"I can believe that." The old man put his hand up to his chin. "Claire should not drink more than one drink. She often forgets the details. Did you forget, Claire?"

Claire blushed. She looked embarrassed. "Papa, you know me too well. Borgia helped me remember."

"Here," I handed the tiara to Claire. "You can have it. I want my dog Eightball, the one Susanna took from me."

"Goodness, first Claire, now Susanna! What will I do about my daughters? Claire, what on earth is going on around here? Missing diamonds, stolen dogs." The old man turned and wagged his finger at her. "We need to get this straightened out right now."

Minutes later, Susanna and Claire's father ushered us into their den. He sank down in a big leather armchair and asked to hear my story. As he listened, he sometimes muttered to himself. The room was full of books. A domed light on his desk glowed like stained glass in an array of colors.

When I was done explaining, he said, "From what you tell me, Eightball definitely belongs to you, Borgia. I provide the majority of funds for Claire and Susanna's projects. I think I can convince Susanna that Eightball—what a strange name—belongs to you."

"He arrived at the shelter with that name," I said.

"Terrible story." The old man shook his head and threw his hands in the air again. "Locked in a crate, set out in a blizzard. It sounds like you and your Aunt Maya saved this dog's life. Susanna, Susanna what will I do with you?"

Claire leaned forward from where she was folded up on the sofa and half whispered to me, "Honestly, my sister is always causing trouble for other people. I heard her tell Maria, Eightball grew too big for her designer dog specifications. Too big to be profitable." My spirits soared at this news, but where was he now? Fear flickered in my chest. I tried to squelch it.

"Hmm," the old man said, obviously overhearing his daughter's comments, "Is Eightball too big for you, Borgia?"

I shook my head. "I love big dogs."

"Finally, some good news," the old man said. " It sounds like Susanna has already changed her mind about keeping this dog, and Claire, you have your tiara back."

Remy suddenly piped up for the first time. "If Borgia's mom is still in trouble with the police because of a diamond theft, will you help clear her name?" All eyes fell on Remy as he shifted uncomfortably in a straight-back chair.

"Absolutely," the old man said. "Claire, you need to call the police first thing tomorrow. Tell them it was a misunderstanding, a mistake, take some responsibility."

"I can do that." Claire smiled wanly. "Where is that crown, anyway? I've already lost it." I pointed between the cushions near her foot where the wedged diamonds sparkled. She laughed.

"It's getting late." The old man glanced at his watch and stifled a yawn. "Do you children need a ride home?"

"No," Remy and I both said hastily, at exactly the same time.

"My cousin is waiting to drive us home," Remy added. "We should get going."

I glanced at Remy and felt my cheeks flaming–poor Lump stuck all this time in the truck with Bello. It dawned on me I had caused all this turmoil by riding a horse across the bridge, and I still had no idea where Eightball was. I felt confused. Eightball was missing, but supposedly Susanna's father would help me get him back.

We stood up to leave. Claire's father handed me a small business card printed with his name and phone number. He repeated he would personally locate Eightball. This was the most promising information of the evening, but there had been so many ups and downs during the last few days–first wild hope, then disappointment–and all without laying an eye on my beloved dog. I crammed the business card into my pocket but checked often to make sure it was there. This little business card was all the hope I had left.

CHAPTER

THIRTY-FOUR

We ran all the way back to the truck stumbling, even bumping into a blue tarp near a foot bridge where two homeless folks screamed as if we were ghosts. "Sorry," we yelled and kept running.

"Amazing night," Remy said breathlessly, when we finally reached Lump.

"Yeah," Lump placed his headphones in his lap. "I've listened to Pink Floyd's *The Wall* a couple times." Then he rolled his head back and forth as if his neck hurt. I could tell waiting in the truck for such a long time was not that great, even if Lump didn't complain.

Remy and I hopped into the cab, and Lump drove back to the animal shelter around the end of the lake without having to go over a bridge. Crammed up against the door, I listened to Bello snorting and shifting in the back, and then I fell asleep.

When I awoke, I had a cramp in my leg, and my cheek ached from being pressed against the window. The first thing I did was pull out the creased business card Susanna's father had handed me. It said, Giuseppe Cavalli, Board of Directors, Trillium Circuits. "How do you say this word?" I spelled the word, "G-i-u-s-e-p-p-e."

Remy shook his head. "Not sure, sounds Italian, but I do know Trillium is a tech company." I slipped the card back into my pocket. A dull ache made me wonder what had just happened.

When we finally got back to Remy's, I made sure Bello was safely secured in his stall with a fresh bed of straw and plenty of oats and alfalfa hay. Then Lump drove me back to the shelter. Maya had locked the front door, so I crawled in through the flip-flop, just like I had on Christmas Eve. She was sitting in her recliner, bleary eyed, cradling a mug of tea. She was so happy to see me, she broke into tears. I felt terrible.

From his perch over the washing machine, Typhoon yelled, "Dirty girl, dirty girl." This time I deserved it. I was filthy. Somehow, I managed to crawl up to bed without waking all the dogs and fall sound asleep on top of the covers. I didn't even wash my face or brush my teeth.

The next morning at breakfast, I tried to explain everything. I showed Maya the business card, but her focus was on me, not Eightball. She made me promise never to run away again. Then Mr. Will stepped into the kitchen and set a copy of *The Seattle Times* on the table. He pointed to the grainy front-page photograph of a girl riding a horse across the floating bridge. The headlines practically shouted, " MYSTERY GIRL RIDES HORSEBACK ACROSS THE BRIDGE." The article went on to question whether Microsoft or Amazon were involved. The paper quoted the crusty bridge guard Gary who insisted the ride was a stunt promoted by one of the giant tech companies.

The article continued, "Godiva Girl, who are you? Anybody recognize this kid? How about the horse? No company claims to have any connection to the stunt, but the bridge guard believes there is a movie crew involved. The plot thickens, the mystery deepens."

Maya pulled her glasses down over the bridge of her nose, as she alternately peered intently at the photo and glared at me. "Borgia, is that you?" I nodded, and she clicked her teeth anxiously, something she only did when she was upset. "We need to call the police right away."

"OK," I said, and she did.

After talking to the police, Maya called my school, then *The Seattle Times*. The landline phone started ringing and did not stop. After cleaning the kennels, Mr. Will stuck his head in the back door and asked, "Want me to answer some of those calls?"

Maya nodded. She looked relieved. The rest of the week was a blur. Mr. Will walked round and round the shelter, answering the phone and talking, talking, talking. Soon, reporters were crawling over the shelter grounds like an infestation of ants. The photos of me crossing the bridge on horseback went viral on social media. The grainy photo seemed to inspire dialogue about what it meant to be an independent girl. I admit I did not really understand.

News reporters appeared in the shelter driveway and on the forest trails. Halo the Great Pyrenees, protector of goats and sheep, barked and barked, standing guard in the pasture. No one tried to take a picture next to him. One reporter did appear on the six o'clock news standing next to Bello, feeding him a carrot.

The news agencies ran stories like, LOCAL GIRL DARES WORKERS TO STOP HER and NO BARRIERS CAN STOP BORGIA.

"Maybe those construction men placed some barriers in your way, maybe not," Maya announced skeptically. "I think Susanna and all her money is the real barrier, not bridge workers." I shrugged. I just wanted Eightball back.

The surveillance shots of me on a horse continued to strike nerves and cause investigations into our lives. The image of Bello jumping over the plastic barricades, as men in hard hats tried to prevent us, was pinned up in college dorm rooms and on office bulletin boards. Maya downloaded copy after copy. She even pinned a photo on the refrigerator. The more I stared at the grainy photo, the less it looked like me. I resembled some fictional character who did not exist. Had I really ridden a horse across the longest floating bridge in the world? Hard to believe, while I stood in front of the refrigerator eating a blueberry muffin.

The phone continued to ring nonstop. Maya and I were invited to appear on talk shows. She turned down most of the TV appearances until someone told her she could also bring a stray dog and try to find it a home. After those first dogs appeared on TV, donations poured into the shelter. A crowd-funding site was started to make sure Bello was well cared for. It even included money for Eightball to be purchased and returned to me. Letters to the editor discussed designer dog breeds and purebred pet ownership. Everyone seemed to agree, Eightball belonged with me, not Susanna, who was nowhere to be found and could not defend herself.

When the driverless car photos surfaced, Lump and Remy were discovered. Both were hailed as future tech engineers and offered student internships at Google and Microsoft over the summer. Lump chose Google. Remy chose Microsoft.

To Maya's delight, social media began to hash over stories of pet neglect and puppy mills. Then the discussion moved on to my early life, with Instagram discussions like, "Where did the name Borgia OftheGlades come from? What connection does Borgia have to the Eastman Johnson painting, *The Girl I Left Behind Me*"?

The Arrowridge Elementary principal reminded all faculty

members not to speak to the reporters about me or any of the students without parental permission. The school secretaries quickly created permission forms, so parents and students could be interviewed legally. Many chose to appear on TV. Kimberly was first and appeared on a local talk show. She wore her plaid skirt with the safety pin sporting five glass beads from the Italian island of Murano. She said I would soon be invited to join the Crisscross Club. She also managed to display her *Spring into the Future Workbook*, letting it be known, she was the only student in the class who completed it. She agreed she loved dogs. Her dog was pure-bred Havanese and only boarded at the Pampered Pets Purebred Spa.

Unfortunately, I was required to attend school counseling sessions to squelch my rebellious streak. Mrs. Dimelroot reported she had been aware of my aberrant personality all along. I watched as she strode down the hall, her nose primly in the air. Mr. McNulty countered her alarmist view by stating any parent would be proud to have an independent child like me. Fortunately, my counseling sessions were with Miss Kinsman, the young woman Mr. McNulty had inadvertently hit with his shoe at the library meeting, his first day back from Canada. Miss Kinsman and Mr. McNulty were dating. Both convinced me, I was a good person and would lead a successful life.

"Is it true you lived in a houseboat blown to bits by fireworks?" a reporter asked me. Invitations arrived to feature my story online in both *Hello* and *People* magazine. I realized that Mom had no idea of all this commotion, because like Susanna, she was overseas. Mom was playing in a series of concerts in Germany. She texted me that cell phone coverage overseas was expensive. Maya said I should wait until she arrived home before I shared my wild bridge adventure. She said it would upset Mom to know her daughter had been riding a horse on the freeway let alone across the Lake Washington floating bridge.

As the weeks wore on, reporters began to portray Maya as an eccentric dog whisperer. She loved the drama, and prior to photo shoots, made sure her hair was as frizzed as possible. She cut up her black bathrobe with the embroidered cherries and green leaves, fashioning it into an odd cape that made her look like a sorceress. Typhoon added to the exotica by perching on her shoulder and shouting "dirty girl" to the world.

Susanna, still in Europe when all the ruckus broke out, was labeled by the media, as a dog owner with no heart. No one had been able to reach her because, as her sister Claire explained, she was at a secluded countryside retreat where you signed a vow of silence and placed your cell phone in a vault for the duration of your stay. Claire said Susanna had agreed not to speak to anyone outside the spa until her stay was over.

In an interview for the evening news, the bridge guard Gary, who had tried to stop Borgia by yelling and shining his flashlight, complained that in these high-tech times, information got scrambled, easily bent out of shape. He said he was glad he planned to retire; his job was more difficult than ever and almost obsolete since the guard tower was to be dismantled, but of course the bridge authority officials were lucky to have him while they worked on the bridge.

He rehashed how he had hoped to have a quiet night eating Top Pot Doughnuts. In his honor, the bakery created a 520-bridge confection with candy corns made to resemble traffic cones, topped off with a drizzled orange frosting that resembled the netting. Gary ordered four dozen doughnuts and sent one to the dog shelter.

"I can tell you everything that happened that night," Gary said. I can give you the truth, the ins and outs of bridge management, maybe even float a TED talk. I know Lake Washington, like nobody else in the whole world," he bragged. "I spent thirty years looking out from the guard tower on the largest, please underline this part, <u>the largest floating bridge in the world</u>."

Back at the shelter, Mr. Will had a knack for managing the numerous reporters who surfaced at the shelter, and his wife Danielle kept tabs on those who wandered into the pasture where Bello grazed.

"When will these 15 minutes of fame be up?" Remy and his mom both asked, after three relentless weeks of strangers tramping around their home, clumping up on the front porch, even trying out the wooden rocking chairs. Eventually a few reporters tromped up and down the lawn outside Remy's private school and took pictures of themselves at the Arboretum with the floating bridge in the background

Lump retreated to the basement, ignoring the hullabaloo. He refused to give interviews, except to Google. The shelter dogs, meanwhile, were going hoarse from all the wild barking they felt obligated to perform.

CHAPTER
THIRTY-FIVE

Then one day there was no more barking. All the dogs up for adoption had found homes. Only a small core of animals remained, the ones Maya could not bear to part with, like Nemo the Newfoundland and Halo the Great Pyrenees. Nemo's desire to remain permanently in a forever home was finally honored, and with special slip covers, he was finally allowed to sleep on the sofa and drink out of the toilet. Halo, as usual, was mostly concerned with protecting sheep and goats in the pasture.

"You are safe here," Maya told Nemo as he sadly watched other dogs leaving. Panting nervously, the great black dog looked from Maya to Mr. Will as if to ask, "Am I next?"

Mobley the mastiff mix was the last to leave, adopted by two nuns who hoped he would wander about the convent, looking fierce. "He's so gentle," they confided to Maya over the phone, "and quite godly." Apparently, the huge dog was thrilled that every evening the nuns encouraged him to sit between them on the sofa and watch *Jeopardy*.

Crumpet the pug mix was adopted by a vegetarian reporter. Always averse to greens, Maya knew there was now little danger of Crumpet overeating. Slider the wedge-faced dog, so fierce and protective, was adopted by Hal, a forest ranger who lived at the top of Snoqualmie Pass. He needed a watchdog to keep bears and bobcats from breaking into his cabin while he was out patrolling for wildfires. Gabriella, a news anchor at King 5 adopted a pair of cream-colored fluff dogs, naming them Gem and Ostia. She texted, she had set matching dog beds in the picture window of her 30th floor condo with a view of Mt Rainier.

A pair of Jack Russells were also adopted together. A computer tech at Facebook said the duo were perfect to patrol along the top of the sofa, barking out the window to discourage squirrels and cats from messing with his bird feeders. Marcy a yoga instructor adopted the basset hound, Deville and allowed her to meander through class–tail high in the air, long ears dragging. Eventually, the basset usually curled up on a pink yoga mat, holding her folded hound configuration for hours of namaste snoozing.

One of my all-time favorite dogs, Metzy the mother of the eight puppies, was adopted by a family with three little girls who adored and spoiled her. Her eight pups had already found homes the minute they were weaned.

Unfortunately, no one wanted the terrible cockatoo Typhoon, especially after hearing him chant "dirty girl" on TV. I thought about all the dents Typhoon had made in the kitchen cupboard doors as he pulled himself around by his beak. I knew there was a long list of reasons not to adopt this crazy parrot. Maya said he had some good points. I disagreed. Hurry Harry the hamster had gone missing again, and Greet the arrogant cat had no intention of leaving his catwalk.

After all the adoptions, Maya and I agreed the shelter was oddly quiet. The fact that Eightball was still missing made the silence even more alarming. I also continued to miss Mom, who apparently had no idea Maya and I were all over the local news.

Just when it appeared the dog shelter would be empty forever , word came from a sister shelter in the Midwest that a senile elderly couple had been hoarding over 30 neglected dogs. Maya was contacted and agreed to accept six. She eagerly awaited word of their flights to Seattle. The Los Angeles Humane Society also contacted her. So many dogs had recently been picked up wandering the LA freeway that all their shelters were overflowing. As usual, Maya was eager to help.

Every time stray dogs were the topic of conversation, I thought about Eightball. Where was he? Susanna's dad called and talked to Maya several times, but had been unable to break through his daughter's vow of silence at her European Spa. "I'm determined to find Eightball and will not give up," he insisted. So I still had hope.

Of course, I wondered where Mom was too. Then a miracle happened. It was a typical Seattle day—light grey clouds, with a mist of moisturizing rain. Often on rainy days, the sun broke through even if only for an hour. Clouds parted and golden light beamed down. Color returned—blue sky, green trees. Windows glimmered, and the world smiled. After school, in just such a burst of sunlight, I walked into the kitchen, plopped my backpack down on a chair and almost tripped over two black garbage bags bound with red ties. Could it possibly be true? Mom always traveled with garbage bags. Just then, Maya rounded the corner and said, "I have a surprise. Let me rephrase that. We have a surprise," and just like that, Mom stepped into the kitchen.

"Mom," I yelled, and hurled myself into her arms.

As usual, Mom was pretty cool. "Hi, Borgia." She held me at arm's length and examined me from head to toe. "You seem to have grown six inches while I was gone. Have I been gone that long?"

"Yes, you have." I grinned. "I've outgrown all my clothes and my shoes too." She shook her head and quickly changed the subject back to herself.

"Maya invited me to stay here a little until I find a place in Seattle."

"Hurrah!" Now I threw myself at Maya, who actually hugged me back.

Mom looked down at her empty hands. "Obviously, I can't stay here in the sticks forever, but a visit will be good for Maya and me to reconnect." Her confident words did not match her expression. She looked tired and humbled, not the loud complaining mom I was used to, nor the proud expert on every-thing under the sun. I felt sorry for her.

Is Del joining you?" I asked.

"No," Mom said brusquely. My brow furrowed. "Why not?" As soon as I spoke, I wished I hadn't. Mom blinked, then looked out the window. She had a long history of breaking up with boyfriends. "I know I am a handful," she often said to Del, and Del liked to repeat that comment. " You are quite a handful, Celia," he'd say sweetly. "I like you that way, but just saying."

"It's all right, Mom. I'm so glad you are here. I missed you." Mom's face softened. She looked up at me with a wry, half-smile. It was true. I was happy. Mom was back. Remy was just a drone flight away. My school was just down the hill, a place where I had real friends and a teacher who thought I was smart. I sat down at the kitchen table and poured myself a big glass of cold milk while Mom and Maya chatted, two sisters reconnect-ing. Mom did most of the talking, lots of complaining. I grinned at her and swung my feet under the table. My world was pulling together.

Mom seemed to get upset when we told her about all the

publicity I received when I tried to rescue Eightball. She agreed with Maya that riding a horse across the Lake Washington Floating Bridge was a risky undertaking, not a solution. It had not brought my dog back. I sighed.

"Agreed," I said, over and over. "I should have waited. I should have consulted an adult." What else could I say?

"Borgia is rather famous for that bridge ride," Maya said, in her supportive way. "A lot of money was raised for the shelter because of the photos." Mom shook her head in disbelief. "The school principal is especially interested that Borgia use her newfound fame to set a good example by cautioning other students about risky behavior." Mom looked at me. I took a big gulp of milk and nodded.

"I am trying to be good," I said. Mom frowned as if she didn't believe me.

Maya nodded supportively. "Borgia is actually doing very well in school."

"Let's not talk about school right now," Mom said. I knew the subject of school was a sore point between the two of them.

Because Susanna remained incommunicado in Europe, no one could figure out the whereabouts of Eightball–not The Pampered Pet Purebred Spa, not Susanna's attorney John Dice, not her sister Claire, not even her father Giuseppe.

Finally, Maria, the maid, dropped a clue that was featured on a local TV special titled "*Where is Eightball?*" Hounded for days by reporters, she finally stopped to answer one question, just as she was about to drive her blue compact through the electronic gate of Susanna's secluded neighborhood. Leaning out the window, she said directly into the camera, "Susanna placed Eightball in a new home. It's permanent." Then she drove away, only deepening the mystery.

When I heard that, I fell into despair. How could my dog have another home? People called Maya and asked if there was a reward if Eightball was located. Hundreds of folks had seen black Lab mixes. Labrador retrievers apparently were the most popular breed in America. Seattle literally had thousands of black dogs matching Eightball's description.

I was kept pretty busy at school and could not focus on Eightball as much as I liked. Mei Ling and I started exchanging notes again, but now that Mei Ling had her own cell phone too, we moved on to texting and never really went back to paper. I saw Remy on the weekends and in the evening. I was fascinated listening to Mom and Maya talk, even argue, about the events of their childhood.

I finally had a chance to ask Mom about the origin of my last name OftheGlades. She told me I was responsible for coming up with that name. When I was three, I could not pronounce my father's last name correctly, and OftheGlades popped out of my mouth and became my name. She also told me I was born in Florida near the Everglades. That news made me happy. All this time I thought I was telling a tall tale that I came from the Everglades, but I really was born in Florida. I had been telling the truth all along.

"How about my real age, Mom?" Maya raised her eyebrows. She looked more disapproving than I had ever seen her.

"Borgia needs to have access to her birth records, Rosy," she added.

"Don't call me Rose. I go by Celia now," Mom huffed.

Maya stood up and clattered around the kitchen putting away dishes, ignoring Mom's cross words.

"Never mind my age," I said, trying to keep the peace. "Sometimes I feel like I'm nine. Other times I feel practically eleven. I'm pretty sure I am around that age range. Remy is twelve. He definitely seems older.

"Why does age matter? Numbers, numbers, numbers,"

Mom said. "Of course, Borgia has a birth certificate. I will locate it, but I can't do everything at once."

Wow, I had a birth certificate somewhere. Someday I would know my real birthday, my exact age.

Maya made no comment. She pulled a pan of piping hot cinnamon rolls out of the oven, and we sat together at the table and ate them as if we were a happy family. Hey, we were a happy family.

CHAPTER
THIRTY-SIX

Mom often mentioned the night she was led away in handcuffs by the police—even though she was released, and there was no evidence of a crime. She seemed worried the police might still come for her. As far as I could tell, she had not broken any laws. I was the one dancing on the stage at the Crocodile Music Hall. I was the one who put the diamond crown in my wicker suitcase. Therefore, I was the one who should be punished. Still, she worried. Unfortunately, one day her shrill terror-stricken voice shattered the silence. "Borgia, the police are here! Help me hide."

"What?" I glanced out my bedroom window. Mom was right. Two police cars were parked in Maya's driveway, their blue lights spinning.

"Stay put," I yelled. "I'll check things out." Maya was in town stocking up on dog food, so I stormed down the stairs, surprised to see Giuseppe Cavalli step out of the squad car. Two policemen followed him, both grinning. I immediately recognized Joe and Clark, the two officers who had searched for Eightball in Remy's barn, ultimately taking him away from me.

"Hello Borgia," Susanna's father said. Even though it was a

warm spring day, he was wearing the same frayed sweater he wore on the night I met him.

"Hi," I said, crossing my arms, worried about what Mom might say and do in the presence of the police.

"Hi, famous Borgia OftheGlades," Officer Joe said cheerfully. Suddenly, I felt as nervous as Mom. I frowned and took a step backward, just as Officer Clark opened his passenger door, and to my amazement, out bounded Eightball. He ran straight to me and hit me with a giant paw.

"Eightball!" I tried to grab him, but he broke free and tore around the shelter. He had grown almost as big as Nemo, but not quite. He wore a new red collar with lots of metal tags.

Officer Joe leaned down and shook my hand. "Sorry we had to arrest your dog. Wanted to make sure we brought him back to you. Enjoy. Gotta run." He turned on his heels and spoke over his shoulder. "Always a busy day for cops. No time to chat."

Officer Clark flashed a big smile. As he pulled open the car door, Eightball made a mad dash for it. "No, no, you don't, big boy. You stay here this time." Clark pushed him away, and I quickly grabbed his collar. I did not know what to say. Eightball was so friendly; it seemed he would leave with anybody who offered him a ride.

Susanna's father broke the silence. "Thanks, fellas, appreciate your help. My driver should be here shortly." Once the police drove away, he turned to me and said, "Do you remember me?"

I nodded. "Susanna and Claire's father. You promised you would find Eightball and you did. Do I get to keep him?"

"He's yours, Borgia."

I clapped my hands. "Thank you so much, Mr. Cavalli."

"Call me Giuseppe," he said, stepping carefully over the uneven pavement in the driveway. "There only a few complications. I want to discuss with you and Maya. I'm also hoping you will give me a tour of the shelter."

"Of course." I also explained that my mom was in the kitchen and at the moment, the only adult at the shelter. Giuseppe smiled and said he would like to meet her. I showed him around the kennels but kept him away from all the crazy dogs that might jump on him. I pointed out Halo the Great Pyrenees standing in the pasture. Giuseppe seemed most impressed by Typhoon the cockatoo raising and lowering his head feathers as he paced back and forth above the washing machine. "Wonderful shelter," he said. " Fun and a bit crazy, seems like a good fit for you." He smiled. "I try to imagine you riding a horse across the Lake Washington Floating Bridge. You are a risk taker, Borgia."

"It was scary. I almost gave up."

"Never give up," Giuseppe said. "I understand you like school. Is that right?"

"Mostly." The giant *Spring into the Future* workbook fluttered its thousand pages in my mind. "Not all assignments, though."

"Maya and I have talked on the phone," Giuseppe said. "She is so proud of your progress."

"She has been very good to me." I ushered Giuseppe into the kitchen and introduced him to Mom. She did not smile and would not shake Giuseppe's outstretched hand. I could tell she did not trust a man who stepped out of a police car.

Giuseppe seemed perfectly comfortable, regardless. "Let me tell you both about the complications surrounding Eightball." He turned to include Mom who had barely acknowledged him. "Keep in mind I am working on a solution."

I slid into the kitchen nook and folded my hands. Giuseppe sat down across from me. Mom stayed standing, leaning against the far counter near the sink. She looked like she might bolt out the door at any moment.

Giuseppe cleared his throat, "Susanna arrived home from Europe last Friday. We got everything straightened out. To her defense, she deals with so many dogs, she doesn't always make the best choices. Unfortunately, she can be appear quite heartless. Eightball just kept growing until he was too big for her designer specifications. When she received a call from the Veteran's Hospital looking for service animals to train with wounded soldiers, she instructed Maria to arrange some transfers and Eightball was included.

"The Veterans rename all the donated dogs. Eightball's new name is Valor, probably why the TV journalists had such a hard time trying to locate him. There are thousands of mixed-breed, dogs in Seattle. As you already know, black being such a common color, made Eightball all the more difficult to trace. Susanna's vow of silence in Europe didn't help things either." I nodded.

"In the meantime, a local high school girl volunteered to help care for Eightball and began training him to become a wounded warrior's service animal. Her name is Careena. She's a gem and fully accepts that Eightball belongs to you because of a mistake."

At that moment I did not like Careena one bit. I tried to rein in my emotion. I bit my lip and swung my feet under the table. Giuseppe did not seem to notice.

"The Veteran's Administration has invested a great deal of time and energy into your dog. He shows great potential as a service animal. He enjoys the training. Still, the Veterans Service Center has agreed to relinquish him back to you, Borgia. Their one request is that Careena be allowed to finish her training with him, as she is learning too. It means Eightball will need to spend two more months at the Veteran's Center in Seattle. Once the training is complete, it would be up to you, whether you still want to keep him or perhaps donate him to the center, where he would be paired with a wounded veteran. You get to decide."

Donate my dog! I hated the idea. I don't think so. Plus, right now, I lived at the animal shelter. How could Eightball possibly be with me and also at the Veteran's Center? Mom spoke up before I could. "How could this possibly work?"

Giuseppe smiled and raised a knowing finger. "Glad you asked. Sounds complicated, no? After conferring with Maya on the phone, we hatched a plan. As it happens, one of my duplexes is only a block away from the Training Center, and there will be an apartment vacancy the end of this month. It's a ground level unit with a small, fenced back yard. I could let you live there rent free until Careena's training is complete. The best news is the apartment is within busing distance to Arrowridge Elementary. Borgia, you could continue to attend your local school."

I watched Mom's face brighten for the first time since she had come to reside at the shelter. I knew she did not like living at the kennel with all the dogs. She and Maya were doing tolerable being together, but neither one really appreciated the lifestyle of the other. Plus, Mom said she was allergic to animal hair, and she still seemed to think Maya was bossing her around.

I perked up too. "I like the idea. Mom and I could live together again in our own space."

Giuseppe smiled, "I thought you would like it."

"What's the catch?" Mom asked, a bit rudely. "Nobody lets people stay rent free." Mom was sounding more like the mom I remembered, a little combative, ready to challenge everyone and everything.

"Good point. Actually, I owe your daughter a favor. I want to repay her for saving Susanna's misplaced pup and also for returning my daughter Claire's diamond tiara."

"What?" A shocked expression darted across Mom's face. "Borgia, did you take the tiara? The one the police thought Del and I stole?"

"I thought it was a gift to me. I had no idea the diamonds were real. Claire put it on my head and said it should belong to me, but it was so scratchy, I slipped it into my wicker suitcase while she was asleep. I didn't want her to think I didn't like it."

Mom seemed stunned. For once in her life, she was at a loss for words.

"Borgia returned the tiara," Giuseppe said. "Mystery solved."

Mom studied me for few seconds as if I were crazy, then she turned to Giuseppe.

"Where is this free apartment located?"

"Half a block from the Veteran Training Center in north Seattle. I knew that news would cinch the deal. Mom was dying to get back to the city.

By the time Maya pulled up with a truck load of dog food, Mom and I had agreed to Giuseppe's plan to move into his duplex. As Eightball panted and turned circles in the kitchen, I gloried in the fact that Mom and I were going to be together again. Mom might be a handful, but she was the only mom I had. Maya seemed undone by the news that we were both leaving. She looked sad and tired, but she perked up when I promised to volunteer at the shelter and even spend some weekends with her.

A few days later, Giuseppe led me into a grey concrete building with an American Flag fluttering overhead in the breeze. A tall girl with short brown hair and a gentle smile greeted us in the entryway. She was dressed casually in jeans and sneakers.

"Borgia, this is Careena. Careena, Borgia." Giuseppe watched us both closely with his calm expression.

To my surprise, I liked Careena immediately. She was warm and friendly and as it turned out, unusually kind. She smiled brightly at me and said, "Borgia, I am so happy to meet you. You raised the most amazing dog." Then she gave me a big hug.

As we walked down the hall, she told me all about her volunteer work. She said part of her job was to pair "wounded warriors" with service animals who could make their lives easier. When we entered the training area, Eightball ran forward and greeted both of us wagging his tail. Then as I watched him follow Careena's commands to sit and lay down, I felt a streak of jealousy.

Still, I was impressed by all the tasks she had taught him to perform. Should he become a real service dog? No, No, and No, I told myself. Would I perhaps change my mind? New ideas were coloring my life. I had been so sure Eightball was mine forever. Now I wondered.

Mr. McNulty said sometimes bad things happen that put us on a better path. I thought about his words often. Mr. McNulty liked to read us stories where the characters suffered but came through in the end. These stories, with sad events, made more sense to me now as I watched Eightball responding to Careena.

Giuseppe said very little while we were at the facility. Afterwards, he took me out for ice cream and talked about Susanna and Claire's projects. He did not ask me what I thought about the Service Center or Careena. I was grateful. I needed time to think.

Our new apartment was on a busy street with noisy traffic, blinding streetlights and blinking crosswalks. Mom loved the location. It was on the edge of the loud, vibrant city and only a short drive to her music venues and friends. Del even came to visit. It felt like old times. If Mom was happy, I was happy.

Eightball stayed with us part of each week. Unfortunately, the back yard was too small for his huge body, and he often barked when he heard loud noises. He started digging holes to pass the time and pulled out some of the shrubs and ripped them to pieces. I had to clean up his poop. Mom thought his long hair made her sneeze.

My bedroom looked out at a small backyard and over the fence into another five-story apartment complex. Now that I had a taste of living in the country, I was feeling partial to views of trees and goats, rather than concrete and bricks. My ideal home would probably always be the houseboat on the water. Mom said our rental houseboat didn't completely sink after all. The owners had renter's insurance that covered the damage. Once the houseboat was repaired, the owners decided to move in themselves. Mom said living on a houseboat was a once in a lifetime experience. Somehow, she had convinced the owner that the near sinking was not her fault.

Now that Susanna was finally back in Seattle, she surprised everyone by scheduling a public meeting with the news media at the Pampered Pet Purebred Dog Spa. Contrary to what one might think, Susanna loved the notoriety surrounding her designer dog ideas and the missing Eightball saga. YouTube videos surfaced of her behind the wheel of her red sports car, lecturing her employees, surrounded by some of Eightball's siblings and also golden doodles and puggles. As I watched her on video, she smiled slyly, carefully placing strands of hair behind her ear to reveal delicate pearl earrings. She seemed to love putting on a display for the camera and did not mind being seen as a villain.

"I grew up on movies and fairy tales," Susanna announced. "Maybe the stories did impact my mindset without my realizing it. I'm no villain, however. I want all my dogs to live glorious lives."

The press managed to get hold of Giuseppe and interviewed him about his early days in Italy. "There was not much to eat after the war," he said, leaning into the microphone. "My parents came to America for a chance at a better life. My girls have that life. I hope they make the best of it and give back to the community. Until then, I am still parenting, as all good fathers should."

CHAPTER

THIRTY-SEVEN

Maya often picked me up on Friday night to spend the weekend. Sadly, Bello was gone, adopted by a single woman who saw him on TV and thought he would be a good trail horse.

Remy was relieved. He no longer had to care for a horse—more time for tinkering on his flying machines. He was always glad to see me, but he seemed more buried in drones and computers than ever. I usually sat and talked to him in the basement while he worked. He said he did not miss Bello at all, but he did miss seeing me. That made me smile.

One Saturday, I was scrolling through text messages at the shelter, when I heard a slight scratching outside my bedroom. Eightball? No, he was training with Careena. I set my phone down and opened the door, surprised to come face to face with one of Metzy's mottled pups. The once fat puppy had stretched out into a young dog. I remembered him best as one of the eight puppies that mobbed me on that fateful night when I first arrived at the shelter.

Thankfully, all Metzy's pups had been adopted, but Maya

told me that one pup had recently been returned when the owner was transferred to New York. This must be the young dog now licking my hand. He obviously remembered me. I hugged him and allowed him to curl up with me on the bed. For the rest of the weekend, he remained glued to my side. If I ignored him too long, I felt a paw. Once he even used his mouth to get my attention, the same way his mother had once pulled me by the wrist to guide me away from the scary dog, Slider.

Maya shook her head when she saw me with the pup. "Dogs seem to belong with you, Borgia. You certainly enjoyed playing with this guy when he was little."

"Metzy's adoption stuck, right?" I often pictured the pup's mother standing between me and the snarling, wedge faced dog. I felt like I owed her my life.

"Yes, Metzy has a forever home. The three sisters adore her, but this poor pup obviously feels abandoned, a little lost, now that all his littermates are gone."

"He's kind of crazy looking," I said, staring at his grey and black mottled coat, "but I love the dark patch over his eye."

Maya leaned over to pet him. "Let's hope Susanna doesn't get her hands on him. She might decide he's her newest designer dog. By the way, his name is Casper."

When Mom picked me up on Sunday, I gave Maya a hug good-bye, then ran back to the house and hugged Casper too.

"You know I can't handle more than one dog," Mom said, watching me through the car window.

For some reason, Mom's comment lingered all day and made me wonder if I could help Casper? I had grown extremely fond of him and had known him virtually his whole life. I owed his mother too. Ugh, the dog situation was getting far too complicated.

The next day, I decided to take Careena up on her offer to

observe Eightball in training. It was always difficult for me to watch how responsive Eightball was to her. True, he still ran and greeted me, but he seemed to enjoy other people just as much.

Careena said young dogs move easily from one owner to another but eventually form a strong bond with their human family. She then introduced me to Cal and Mario. Both were wounded warriors, learning how to work with service dogs to gain access to a better life. Watching them practice with Eightball, I was fascinated.

"You taught Eightball so many skills, Careena."

"He is such a strong positive dog," she said, smiling. "It's difficult to find the right combination of personality—a dog that can sit relaxed for hours, but also participate eagerly in a number of complicated activities without flinching." I nodded. Eightball was special. He enjoyed all the attention too.

As the training progressed, Eightball spent four days a week at the training center. The facility had a huge dog run and a play area where he got to romp with other service dogs.

Cal was now working exclusively with Eightball. I admired his prosthetic hand and realized he probably had other injuries I could not see. As I stood on the sidelines, it was obvious that the two worked well together. At the end of the session, Careena gave Eightball a rewarding pat and told me it was hard for her to part with a training dog, but she knew she had to do it to help a soldier. I steeled myself against those words. Was Cal hoping to keep my dog as his service animal?

My face must have revealed my resistance. "Oh, I don't mean you, Borgia. I know Eightball belongs with you, but the fact that he likes everybody, makes for great training. Cal lost his hand in Afghanistan and has limited mobility, but he's adjusting well to being home. He realizes a service dog will add a dimension to his life that has been taken away from him."

As I stood and watched Eightball obey Cal's commands, my cell rang and Maya's face appeared, staring at me, through her owl-like glasses.

"Borgia, you have to hear this." I listened as Maya clumped up the stairs, huffing and puffing. She aimed her cell phone, and there on my bed sat the mottled pup Casper, his nose in the air, howling miserably.

"What's that about?" I asked, turning down the volume on the horrible sound.

Maya now stared back at me. "Casper misses you. He spends all his time in your room, waiting for you to return. That's all, got to run. Halo is barking at someone on the road. Bye," and the screen went blank.

I walked back into the training room and stood next to Careena. She offered me half a cream cheese bagel. She often shared her lunch with me and had a knack for demonstrating what it meant to give of yourself. I took a bite. I wanted to be more like her.

I pictured sad rejected Casper, a dog I had played with ever since he was a tiny puppy. Maya was tricky, calling me, so I could hear him howling. Thinking about Casper and how to help him, gave me a sudden idea. I wasn't sure of the outcome, but all the possibilities seemed sound. Like the round black eight ball that you ask *yes* and *no* questions for a clear answer, I thought if I carried out my plan, I would discover a yes or no solution to my own problem–my inability to make a decision about Eightball, my beloved dog. I wanted to keep him, but I had to admit Cal needed him more than I did.

"Careena," I said, when my mouth was no longer full of bagel. "I'd like permission to bring a young shelter dog to watch the training. He knows Eightball, so I'm sure he won't be any trouble."

"Of course," Careena said without hesitation. "We are always happy to meet new dogs."

The next training session, I arrived with Casper. Both Maya and I had been working with him, so he already knew basic commands. He sat quietly but could not restrain himself when he saw Eight ball. The two dogs were overjoyed to be together again.

I started bringing Casper to every training session. He followed every move Eightball made. Then one day when I wasn't watching him, he ran to Cal, licked his hand, then sat and stared at him as though awaiting a command.

Cal laughed. "Ok, Casper, want to try and help me?" He gave him several commands and the mottled dog completed each task with perfection. Meanwhile Eightball had returned to my side and was begging for part of my sandwich.

"Amazing," Careena said, watching Casper. "He obviously has learned all the commands just by watching. If it's OK with you I'd like to include him in the training sessions."

"Absolutely!" I replied. My plan was working perfectly.

A few weeks later, Cal asked if there were any possibility he could train exclusively with Casper. Careena said the two had formed such a strong bond, she intended to match Cal with Casper as his personal service animal. "Only if you and Maya approve, of course," she said, smiling.

"Maya will be thrilled." Naturally, I was thrilled too.

Three weeks later Eightball completed his training. "Whenever you leave the room without him, he looks worried," Careena announced. "He has obviously formed a strong bond with you. Eightball belongs at your side." She smiled at me, and those amazing words rang over and over in my mind. "Eightball belongs at your side." I so agreed.

It also meant the world to me, that Careena, a true dog expert, had confirmed our relationship. I loved her idea of strong bonds. Maya still needed me. I was sure of that. I needed her too, almost as much as I needed Mom. The more Mom talked about upcoming concert venues in France, the more I realized I wanted to stay on at the shelter while she was traveling. I was thrilled when Mom agreed with me. That meant more time with Aunt Maya and more time with friends like Remy and Mei Ling, also more time to spend with all the crazy animals. Eightball would love it too. Mom even said, I could keep attending Arrowridge School. Hurrah.

For the first time, so much seemed possible. Maybe Mom would find my real birth certificate, so I could be officially registered at school. I smiled. I no longer felt left behind, and I had no intention of ever leaving those I loved. Eightball might have been a fine service dog, but I knew his home was with me. Casper obviously was perfect to take his place and help Cal. Then Remy called and told me Bello had been returned to their pasture because he kept jumping the fence. "You better plan on more riding," he said.

"You kidding, Remy. I'll be over today." Wow, I could ride horseback again.

Careena added the finishing touch by being my friend and making me feel good. "Look at how Eightball sticks close to you and lets Casper do all the hard work. This has all worked out for the better."

I gave Careena a big hug. "So glad I met you."

She smiled. "You are welcome here at the training center anytime. I plan to visit you at the shelter, meet Maya and all those crazy animals."

I laughed. "Be prepared for lots of commotion, not like the polite dogs here."

As I walked home with Eightball gallantly pulling on his leash, I thought about all the people who had helped me find my way. Careena's kind words kept surfacing and made my heart sing. Eightball and I were back together. Casper had a new life. No one was being left behind, not even me. I loved my mom and was glad she could perform her music. She would always play a big role in my life. In the meantime Aunt Maya and I would do just fine together.

About the Author

Laura Drumheller enjoys walking her dog on the trails near her home where she can glimpse Seattle and the Space Needle from afar. An educator, she has great respect for young people and enjoyed being involved with English and creative writing classes at public high schools in the Seattle area. Founding an Open Microphone program for students to express themselves before an audience of peers was especially rewarding. She loves to read, travel and enjoys spending time with friends and family.

Her poetry has appeared on Seattle Metro buses and in literary magazines. This is her second novel. Her first work, *The Late Great Cakes of the United States,* a young adult, sci-fi fantasy is published under the pen name Peregrine Maxson.

Made in the USA
Columbia, SC
19 January 2026

77699535R00128